THE ODYSSEY OF HANNAH AND THE HORSEMAN

THE ODYSSEY OF HANNAH AND THE HORSEMAN

•

Johnny D. Boggs

AVALON BOOKS
NEW YORK

Published by Thomas Bouregy & Co., Inc.
160 Madison Avenue, New York, NY 10016

PRINTED IN THE UNITED STATES OF AMERICA
ON ACID-FREE PAPER
BY HADDON CRAFTSMEN, BLOOMSBURG, PENNSYLVANIA

For Jeff Rogers,
who helped keep chapters 1–7 from being lost forever
in the Cyberspace Badlands;
and his family: Lisa, Caroline and Abby

Chapter One

"Y̶ou are not kissing me, Petros Belissari."

Hannah Scott stood in the doorway to her second-story room at the Marfa Hotel, hands on her hips, staring at Pete Belissari partly in amusement, but more in shock. Pete had talked Hannah into the trip to the railroad town for the fall dance. She needed to take Cynthia to the dentist here anyway. Well, she could have taken the ten-year-old orphan to Homer Foster, the Fort Davis barber, or let Pete pull the tooth himself. But Marfa had a real dentist, a doctor who had studied in Baltimore, so here they were. Of course, Pete had convinced them to stay overnight, promising to take Hannah to the hotel restaurant, which served meals at any time, before they danced the night away. It was a special treat. Hannah had known Pete for more than two years. They had been dancing once.

So Hannah put Cynthia, sans one bad tooth, to bed

while Pete disappeared into his own room to get duded up. He had shaved, too.

That's why Hannah stared at him so.

Off had come Pete's thick, dark mustache. Earlier in the day, he had let the barber trim his long hair until it barely touched his collar, then spent a chunk of his horse-breaking earnings at S. F. Wiles General Merchandise and Ranch Supplies on a coat and tie. He looked like a prosperous man about Marfa, except for the calf-high Apache-style moccasins he wore. And most businessmen wore their hair a tad shorter.

But the mustache was gone, and Hannah had never seen him without one. For that matter, Pete hadn't seen himself clean-shaven since graduating from the University of Louisville some eight years earlier. Pete had been a tad shocked himself when he stared at his reflection in the mirror.

"*Po po!*" he said in Greek. "I look like my sister!"

Hannah had pretty much the same reaction.

A train whistle cried from the depot. Hannah stared. She wore a baby-blue dress with a stand-up collar and pleated yoke, both trimmed with white lace. Apparently, Hannah had done a little shopping herself. Slowly, she reached out and touched Pete's upper lip as if she were smoothing his mustache. It felt strange. Some men said they felt naked when they walked around without a revolver strapped to their hip. Pete Belissari suddenly felt undressed without his mustache.

"It's me," he said. "I promise."

"It's your voice," Hannah said. "It's not your face."

Pete sighed. He was hungry, and the Marfa Hotel

served up some pretty good grub unless you got on the cook's bad side. Before hiring on with the hotel, Roland Jackson had served as a cook for one of the big ranches near Fort Stockton and never forgot what it was like cooking for a bunch of mule-headed Texas waddies. So if a customer in the Marfa Hotel complained about the service, he just might discover pebbles in his beans. 'Course, that was a tad better than finding out his coffee had been made with day-old grounds and water from the horses's trough out front.

Hannah finally smiled. "You look different."

"More handsome?"

"No, just different." She reached up and gave his cheek a peck. The lips would have to wait, until after a dance or two. Pete offered her his arm, she took it, and the two walked downstairs.

"How is Cynthia?" Pete asked.

"Fine," she answered, staring at his face instead of watching her step. "Asleep." She touched him again. "How does it feel?"

"Different," he replied. "About ten pounds lighter, only I keep going to pull on it, and it ain't there."

"*Ain't?* Pete Belissari, you never say *ain't.*"

He started to answer, but by now they stood on the ground floor. Saturday afternoon in Marfa should be bustling, the hotel crowded. They had heard the train pull up, yet the lobby was empty. Even the desk clerk was gone. A crudely painted sign hung on the doorknob to the restaurant: CLOSD

Pete and Hannah stared at each other for a minute, then walked outside. Black smoke puffed from the locomotive on the edge of town as the engine heaved.

That's where the crowd had gathered. In fact, it looked as though everyone in Marfa stared at the train, keeping a safe distance from the Army guards that surrounded the cattle cars as the doors fell open. Longhorns didn't step out of the vehicles, though. These were men.

Apaches.

"Oh, my," Hannah said.

They walked down the street, pushing their way through the crowd for a better view. A man in a linen duster and high derby kept glancing from a copy of *Harper's Weekly* to the scene in front of him.

"Stretch your legs," one of the soldiers said, and another repeated the order in Spanish.

The Apaches were hard-looking, dirty and tired, dressed in a mix of buckskin and a sutler's wares. Some donned hats, but most had wrapped silk or cotton bands around their heads. Black, glistening hair fell past their shoulders. Belissari spotted rock amulets, Army-issue vests, strange necklaces, bandannas, breechclouts, cotton drawers, pendants, beads, bracelets, and at least one pocket watch. Yet every one wore moccasins; Pete immediately felt self-conscious.

"Which one is he?" a bearded cowboy in mule-ear boots asked the *Harper's Weekly*–carrying gent.

The stranger studied the cover of his journal. A drawing of one Apache on horseback, sided by several warriors, covered the top half of the *Harper's*. The bottom half held another sketch of a desert conference between the Army and the Apaches. "I can't tell," the man said, and jabbed a bony finger at the drawing of a seated Indian at the conference, then searched the faces of the real Apaches before him.

"There," the cowboy said. "How 'bout that buck in the straw hat?"

The gent studied the face, compared it to the *Harper's*, and nodded. "Yeah," he said. "That's got to be him." He whistled. "Geronimo!" He laughed. "You better be glad he's just stopping to stretch his legs, Jim. Else your scalp might be hanging on that old boy's belt."

"Apaches don't scalp." Pete didn't know why he said that. The words just came out. The cowboy and the gent stared at him briefly, then the latter glanced at Pete's moccasins and smiled. "Whatever, Chief," he said, then folded the *Harper's* and nudged his companion. "Come on, Jim, we've seen the old killer. Now let's cut the dust."

Pete looked at the Apache warrior. Long hair hung above his shoulders, and fifty or sixty years of weather and the Southwestern sun had baked and crevassed his dark copper face. He was dressed in white cotton, like some Mexican farmer, with the omnipresent moccasins, a necklace of some sort—bear teeth, maybe?—and a flat straw hat you would expect to find topping the attire of a Louisiana planter, not the most feared Apache warrior since Cochise. Belissari had traded shots with Apaches before, but those had been Mescalero boys who jumped the reservation in New Mexico to steal horses and pretend they were living in the old days. This was Geronimo, who had led a handful of men and women through the Southwest against

Americans, Mexicans, and even other Apaches until this month.

Geronimo and the last of the Chiricahua Apache warriors had surrendered unconditionally to General Nelson Miles in early September and were taken to Fort Bowie in Arizona Territory. Now, the Apaches were being sent East, as prisoners of war, exiled from their homeland to Florida. A feeling of shame had overcome Pete for gawking at the warrior when he noticed the Apache standing just behind Geronimo.

Pete guessed him to be in his twenties, although it was hard to tell. He was tall for an Apache, with a round face and hard black eyes that stared straight through Pete. Belissari couldn't match the Indian's gaze, so he looked away and studied his own feet before summing up the nerve to look at the warrior again. The Apache wore a cloth headband of bright yellow, and a beaded necklace and green bandanna, fastened with a silver conch, around his neck. A tan corduroy vest, completely buttoned, covered a cotton shirt of red-and-white calico, and tin cones decorated the sides of his Army-issue trousers, tucked into his moccasins. He still stared at Pete, hadn't moved, and didn't even appear to be breathing.

Pete shuddered, realizing the Apache wasn't focused on him. He was staring at Hannah.

"Let's go," he said.

She nodded, and they moved back through the crowd, across the depot and onto the dusty boardwalk that led down Main Street to the hotel. The train whistle blared once more, and one of the soldiers called out: "All right, file back onto the train. Now!" As another soldier translated the order into Spanish, Hannah sighed.

"I wonder if this is right," she said softly.

"What's that?"

"Deporting those Indians back East."

Belissari shrugged. "Nothing we can do about it."

"Sometimes, it doesn't seem just. They were fighting for their homeland."

"So were Victorio, Mangas Coloradas, Cochise, all of the Apaches. The same with Joseph's Nez Perce, Crazy Horse's Sioux, Satanta's Kiowa, and a lot more chiefs and tribes. So was the Confederacy for that matter."

Hannah stopped and sat on a bench in front of the mercantile. She smiled up at Pete, and shook her head. "Are you hungry?"

Pete shrugged. He was famished, but that didn't matter. "I don't think anyone's going to eat in this town until that train leaves." He sat beside her. She gripped his right hand, squeezed it gently, and stared across the street but didn't really see anything. Her thoughts remained back on that train with those Apache prisoners.

"I guess I should be excited, like most folks in town," she said after a while. "I mean, how many people can say 'I saw the great Geronimo'?"

"A lot of people lived to regret they could say that."

They sat quietly for a few minutes, enjoying the fall breeze. Clouds gathered in the west. Maybe it would rain. It had been a miserable spring and summer. Pete started to lift his left hand to his face, and almost laughed at himself. *No more mustache,* he thought. He looked at the depot. Marfa's citizens began walking away from the train as the soldiers climbed aboard a trailing flat car and the locomotive grunted and began its journey east toward San Antonio.

"Did you notice that one Indian?" Hannah asked. "The tall one behind Geronimo?"

Pete nodded.

"He was staring right at me."

He tried to think of the right answer. *Probably wants you for a wife. . . . Really? . . . Yeah, I noticed that. . . .* Finally satisfied, he answered, "A lot of men do that, Hannah Scott."

Smiling, she leaned over to rest her head on his shoulder. "You're a sweetheart, Petros, even without your mustache."

He kissed her blond hair and started to whisper something into her ear, when she blurted out, "He had such gentle eyes."

Pete sat up straight.

Gentle? That Apache? Those eyes, black as coal, looked like a pair of stilettos. The warrior seemed like a messenger of Death, which he probably had delivered time and again in Arizona and New Mexico territories, maybe even Texas, not to mention Sonora and Chihuahua south of the border. Pete glanced down the boardwalk and saw the train far away now, growing smaller in the horizon, taking Geronimo and his friend with the "gentle eyes" far away from West Texas, far from Hannah Scott.

Pete felt relieved, but it didn't last long. A chill raced up his back and across his shoulders, causing him to tremble.

"You all right?" Hannah asked.

"Yeah," he said. "Someone . . ." He stopped. The old saying, "Someone stepped on my grave," didn't sound reassuring or funny now. He felt nervous, as if he knew for certain he would stare into those malevolent eyes again.

Chapter Two

A rooster crowed, a dog yelped, and a wagon desperately needing its axles greased screeched its way down Main Street. Hannah opened her eyes, swallowed, and first tried to will the wagon faster so it would take its noise out of town, then prayed for it to stop. And it stopped. Hannah's head pounded. She tried closing her eyes, but the room began spinning around, or maybe only the bed twirled and pitched. Hannah forced her eyelids up, and all movement stopped.

She sighed.

Hannah Scott, the esteemed lady rancher of the Limpia Creek Cattleman's Association, mother figure to a passel of orphans and member of the Fort Davis Presbyterian Church, lay with a brutal headache and queasy stomach, suffering in an uncomfortable bed with a hangover. But how? She had had only one glass of wine with dinner before going to the dance. That was all. The wine had tasted like bitter grapes. A sign proclaiming that *"Intoxicating Liquors Are Forbidden"* greeted them at the barn where the fall dance was in full swing. She tried to forget about her current condition and remember last night's fun. Pete Belissari turned out to be a pretty good dancer. She had stepped on his toes more than he had stepped on hers. The fiddle player from Presidio and the banjo player from a ranch southwest of Marathon kept all the couples busy, with "Oh My Darling Clementine," "The Blue Tail Fly," "Oh! Susanna," "The Bonnie Blue Flag," "Old Zip Coon," "My Old Kentucky Home," "Lorena," "Sweet Betsy from Pike," "Green Grow the Lilacs," "Tassels on My Boots," and some they just made up as they went.

"Mama Hannah?"

Hannah turned delicately to find Cynthia standing over the bed with her face washed and hair brushed. "You're up mighty early," Hannah said, surprised she could speak.

"It's nine, Mama Hannah. Are you sick or something?"

The screeching wagon resumed its skin-crawling trek of torture. Hannah groaned. "I'll be all right. How do you feel?"

Cynthia grinned, stuck a finger in her mouth, and pulled back the corner of her lips, trying to reveal the spot where her tooth had been pulled and saying, "See? It don't hurt one bit." She removed her finger to speak a little more clearly. "I got the bum tooth wrapped up in my pocket. I'm gonna show it off to

Darcy and Paco and them back home, make them jealous."

Hannah thought about smiling, but decided against it. Smiling might hurt. If she had the strength, she would have marched across the room, opened the window, and screamed at the wagon driver. Instead, she looked at the girl.

"Can I go to the livery stable?" Cynthia pleaded. "Just for a few minutes."

"Why?"

"Because Mr. Evans has a beautiful palomino mare. He's asking for two hundred dollars for her, but Pete says he won't get near that much. It's a beautiful horse, Mama Hannah, short-coupled, fourteen hands high. Pete says she's a mighty fine animal. I just want to look at her for a while, talk to Mr. Evans about her. I won't get in the way, and I'll be back in no time at all."

This time, Hannah couldn't help but smile. She remembered back when dolls and penny candy had been Cynthia's foremost interests. Now the girl spent too much time in corrals when she should be burying her nose in schoolbooks. But Hannah couldn't fault the child.

Hannah noticed just how beautiful Cynthia had become. She had always been the prettiest of the orphan children. Only ten years old, she had become an excellent rider under Pete's instructions, sailing along with her auburn hair flowing in the wind as she galloped up and down the San Antonio–El Paso Road that led past their Wild Rose Ranch. She seldom used a sidesaddle, either, despite Hannah's suggestions. "You never use a sidesaddle, Mama Hannah," the girl would respond, to which Hannah had no reply.

"Go on," Hannah told Cynthia, "but be careful and don't stay long."

Hannah cringed as the girl ran across the floor and opened and slammed the door. The room started to spin again. The noise from the wagon got louder.

Why doesn't somebody shoot that madman? Hannah thought.

"Comin' off a wine drunk's the worst feelin' in the world."

Buddy Pecos had spoken those words months before, to one sick cowboy in jail back when Pecos had been Acting Sheriff of Presidio County, but Pete Belissari had known the veracity of that statement long before he met his partner. Pete remembered celebrating a birthday with a friend at the University of Louisville many years ago. Well, Pete actually couldn't remember that much about his birthday night. But he could remember the hangover.

Muscadine wine shipped all the way from Natchez, Mississippi. "Scuppernong," the waiter at the hotel dining room had told them. "Our most popular vintage. A fine drink with your steaks and fried taters." *Liar,* Pete thought now. He'd probably been trying to get rid of that poison for months. They should tar and feather the rogue. The wine went down like tree bark, but he had only polished off one glass. So had Hannah. The rest had remained in the bottle, which Pete left behind in lieu of a tip.

It wasn't the wine, Pete realized as he crawled

slowly out of his bed. The punch! All of those Circle
L boys smiling and standing around the refreshment
table at the dance. They had slipped a little—no, a
lot—of pop skull into the punch. Pete pulled on his
trousers and walked barefoot across the hotel floor,
forced up the window, and watched as the town marshal threatened the driver of a buckboard with what
looked to be a shotgun. The marshal had also been at
the dance, and, as Pete recalled, he had frequented the
punch bowl several times. Something flashed down the
boardwalk. Pete smiled, recognizing Cynthia as she
bolted across town. Having a tooth pulled apparently
couldn't keep her down for long. Pete wondered how
Hannah felt this morning.

The westbound train pulled into the depot, black-
ening the late-morning sky with thick smoke. Pete
watched for a few minutes, filling his lungs with fresh
air, then walked inside the Marfa Hotel, climbed the
stairs, and softly rapped on the door to room 213. After hearing a faint "Come in," he entered Hannah's
room, softly closing the door behind him, and smiled
as she sat up in the bed, positioning the pillows for
back support. Her face seemed pale, her eyes red, and
her hair in need of a hour's work with a curry comb.

"If you say anything, you're a dead man," she
calmly told him.

He had planned to say something like, "I've never
seen you in bed past seven," but he took her advice
and pulled up a chair beside the window, watching the
passengers and locals mill about the depot.

"Want some water?" he asked. She mumbled a no.

"I can bring some coffee up." Another decline. He rubbed his tongue over his teeth, felt his freshly shaven face, looked out the window for a few minutes, and finally remarked, "It was the punch."

"What?"

"The punch. Those waddies spiked the punch last night. It wasn't the wine." He turned to face her.

Finally, she smiled. "I thought you might have been trying to get me intoxicated."

"If that had been the case, I would have chosen a Greek wine, or ouzo."

Hannah laughed, threw off the covers, and swung out of bed. She paused just long enough to let a dizzy spell subside. Pete looked out the window as she disappeared behind a folding wooden partition and began splashing water over her face.

"What time is it?" she asked.

"Ten-thirty-five. I went downstairs looking for you, had some coffee, and the desk clerk said you hadn't come down yet. I figured you must be feeling poorly."

"You figured right. Have you seen Cynthia?"

"Saw her blast down the street earlier this morning, about nine."

"She wanted to go to Clay Evans's livery, look at a horse." Her head appeared above the partition, and she winked. "You're rubbing off on that girl."

If Hannah had begun to feel better, the departing train caused a relapse. The locomotive's shrill whistle provoked an unladylike comment from her. Pete bit his lower lip to keep from laughing. He found a speck of dust rising off in the eastern horizon, coming from Alpine or thereabouts, and concentrated on that for a while, indifferently at first, but as the white dust cloud neared, he became more interested. Several riders galloped toward town, and after a few minutes he could just make out the United States guidon flapping in the wind. Cavalry. Strange, he thought. He hadn't seen an Army patrol riding that hard in a year, probably even longer.

The troopers reined up in front of the depot, and a young officer brushed the dust off his blouse while talking to the town marshal. He recognized the lieutenant as one of Colonel Clendenin's Third Cavalry boys from Fort Davis. But the fort lay north of Marfa, and this troop had ridden in from the east. He didn't know the officer's name. Pete hadn't gotten to know many soldiers at the outpost since he had been forced to quit selling horses to the Army in '84 and his friends with the Tenth Cavalry pulled out a year later. A crowd gathered around the soldiers, civilians and military men gesturing wildly. Pete ground his teeth. This looked like trouble.

"You haven't heard one thing I said, Petros Belissari."

Pete turned, mumbling an apology. "The brush?" Hannah said, nodding toward the dresser. "Please." He moved away from the window and tossed the brush across the room. Hannah caught it, although his aim had been off, and she shook her head.

"What's so interesting outside?" she asked. "Did they hang that wagon driver who made so much noise this morning?"

Pete shook his head and returned to the window.

"Army patrol just rode up," he told her. "I wonder what they want."

Hannah stopped brushing her hair for a minute, contemplated this, and walked toward him. She wore a blue gingham dress and fastened a Saint Christopher medallion around her thin neck. "Lot of excitement," she said.

"Yeah."

Hannah groaned, rubbed her temples, and walked to the chair to button up her shoes. Pete studied the scene at the depot.

The officer had dismounted, removed his battered campaign hat, and ran fingers through stringy white hair. Suddenly, a woman screamed. Hannah spun around, her shoes on but unbuttoned, and looked toward Pete. Outside, a barefoot Mexican youth sprinted to the soldiers and spoke hurriedly. In seconds, the soldiers, marshal, and what seemed like half of town moved away from the depot, heading toward Cal Evans's Livery and Wagon Yard with dutiful purpose.

A man staggered from the barn, wounded in the head, blood drenching the front of his white shirt. The palomino horse that the livery owner had been showing off in the corral was gone. The wounded man collapsed just as the posse reached the livery.

Pete turned to Hannah. "Where did you say Cynthia went this morning?"

"The livery. Why? What is it?"

Pete didn't answer. He forgot about muscadine wine, about spiked punch and hangovers—he even forgot about Hannah Scott this instant—and tore across the hotel room, not even bothering to close the door behind him.

Fearing the worst, Hannah kicked off her shoes and followed.

Chapter Three

Pete shoved his way through the crowd at the livery without apologizing until he made it to the clearing where the town marshal and Army officer squatted by an ashen-faced, blood-soaked Cal Evans.

"Back up, folks! Give us some room here!" a black-mustached sergeant shouted in an Irish brogue. Pete didn't obey. His eyes searched the corral for Cynthia but he couldn't find her. The sergeant put a meaty right hand on Belissari's shoulder. Pete pulled away and started for the livery.

Cal Evans's voice stopped him.

"Pete," he said weakly. "I'm so sorry."

Belissari knelt by the livery owner. His head had been bandaged with the lieutenant's cotton bandanna, which hadn't come close to stanching the flow of blood. This man needed stitches—quickly. The marshal seemed to read Pete's mind.

"Where is Doc Gaston?"

No one answered.

"What happened?" Pete asked.

Evans closed his eyes and sighed. "She was on the top rail of the corral, watching Prancer, that palomino of mine," the weakening man said. "I heard her scream. Started outside, and figured she had slipped off the fence or something. Then I saw him. That black-hearted devil had swung your little girl over his shoulder and was leading Prancer out of the corral. I tried to stop him, charged him. Never saw what he hit me with. Pete, tell Hannah—"

He slumped against the marshal's chest. The lawman spit out a fountain of tobacco juice and swore. "Somebody get that doctor!"

Pete turned to the lieutenant. "Who?"

"The Chiricahuas call him He Who Chops Off The Heads Of His Enemies. We call him Hector, for short."

"An Apache?" Pete remembered the Indian prisoners from the train the day before. His heart sank. Even without being told, he knew Hector: the brave who had stood behind old Geronimo. Yellow headband. Tan vest. The tin cones sewed up and down the yellow stripes on the side of the sky-blue trousers. Those unfeeling black eyes. Hundreds of Apaches had been on that train, but Pete knew this was Hector.

Someone in the crowd shouted, "This is the Army's fault! Now we got a renegade Apache on the loose!"

Another person joined in. "He's practically killed Clay Evans, and now he has that little girl!"

Pete ignored the taunts. So did the soldiers. He looked at the officer and waited for the man to con-

tinue. Man? The lieutenant looked barely old enough
to shave. Even the long white hair failed to make him
look older.

"Hector somehow got out of one of the boxcars at
a water stop last night," the officer said. "We were on
a routine patrol when a galloper reached us with the
news. We tried to pick up the trail, but he moves like
the wind. There had been no sign of him in Marathon
or Alpine, and I thought for certain he couldn't have
reached Marfa by now. I don't understand how he
could move so fast, without a horse."

"He's an Apache, sir," the sergeant said. "And now
he's got a horse."

A good horse, too, Pete thought. And he was carrying Cynthia as a hostage.

The crowd parted. At first Pete thought they were
making room for Doc Gaston, but he looked up to see
Hannah. She moved gingerly across the rocky dirt
with bare feet. Her lips trembled as she studied each
face before her—the soldier, the marshal, Evans, and
finally Belissari.

"Pete," she said unsteadily, "where's Cynthia?"

Someone in the crowd swore. "Blasted Apache has
kidnapped her, thanks to the Yankee army."

He moved quickly now, pushing himself up as her
knees buckled and her eyes rolled back. Pete caught
Hannah underneath her shoulders as she sank heavily.
He glared at the idiot in front of him, the one whose
words had caused Hannah to faint. Belissari wanted to
lash out at the fool—the same man who had been
carrying the *Harper's Weekly* yesterday—but that
would mean letting Hannah drop to the ground. The

sergeant intervened, sending a roundhouse right to the gent's jaw that felled the man instantly.

"If you folks don't back up, and if someone doesn't bring that doctor here in the next two minutes, you Texicans are going to think the last day at the Alamo was a Sunday afternoon picnic. Now move!"

Hannah woke up back in her hotel room. She rarely fainted, and almost cursed herself for doing so now, in front of half the town. *Cynthia,* she thought, and tears welled in her blue eyes. The dance, the stupid hangover . . . they all seemed to have happened ages ago. She felt the damp rag on her forehead, picked it up, and threw it across the room. It hit the far wall with a splat, stuck there for half a minute, then dropped to the hardwood floor.

Pete opened the door, saw that she was awake, and pulled up a chair beside the bed.

"The Army patrol pulled out an hour ago," he said. "A posse is forming in town. I'm going with them. We'll get her back, Hannah, I promise."

"I'm going with you," she said.

"Hannah." Pete inhaled, then let his breath out slowly. He had lost this argument hundreds of times before. "All right."

She blinked back tears, shook her head as if to send all emotion away, and sat up. Resolve failed her, though, and she cried, leaning on Pete's shoulder as he stroked her hair, kissed her softly, and told her everything would be fine.

"Listen," he said. "Apaches don't hurt young captives. They don't abuse women or girls. This is one man. Alone. He has nowhere to go. The government's sending all of the Apaches out of Arizona Territory, so it's not like he can find some band and hide out in a stronghold. Texas Rangers, local posses, and U.S. and Mexican troops are already on the trail. He doesn't even have a gun. And Cynthia can take care of herself. She can outride any Apache. Heck, she's probably bushwhacked him and is riding that palomino mare home right now."

Hannah pulled away, wiped her eyes, and tried to smile. "Maybe she figured that's the only way she could get that horse." The smile disappeared. Her joke failed. She cried again, only harder.

He Who Chops Off The Heads Of His Enemies had been born in the Mogollon band of the Chiricahua Apaches. They ranged from southwestern New Mexico Territory into northern Mexico. He had taken part in Nana's bloody two-month-long raid in New Mexico back in '81 and disappeared into Sonora. Later he returned to the San Carlos agency in Arizona, and enlisted in Gen. Crook's unit of Apache scouts.

So He Who Chops Off The Heads Of His Enemies took to the white man's road and helped his former enemy track down his friends and family. "Wolves," the hostile Apaches called them. But Crook's plan seemed to work, and He Who Chops Off The Heads Of His Enemies gained a reputation as an excellent, though brutal, scout. Chief of Scouts Al Sieber shortened the Apache's name to Hector.

The Army had betrayed Hector and all of the Apache scouts, though, after Geronimo's surrender. It

didn't matter that the scouts had played an integral part
in the end of Apache hostilities in Arizona and New
Mexico. They were all Indians, all enemies of the
white race, so Apache scouts and Apache hostilities
had been loaded on the trains in Holbrook and shipped
East as prisoners of war.

Pete had learned this from Sgt. Quincannon and Lt.
Hammond before the cavalry troopers rode toward the
Rio Grande. Belissari couldn't blame Hector for es-
caping the prisoner of war train. He could even understand the warrior's reasoning for kidnapping
Cynthia. Holding a captive would make his pursuers
think twice. Had Pete been in the same situation . . .
No, he decided, he would never put a ten-year-old
child in harm's way.

He had been honest with Hannah, though. Apaches
might whip their young captives to force them to
work, but they wouldn't kill them. They might torture
an adult male captive but not children. They didn't
scalp their enemies. In many ways, Pete found the
Apaches to be a fascinating, civilized culture. They
reminded him of ancient Greek warriors. But Hector
had also been with the white men for a long time. He
had learned the meaning of lies and betrayal. Maybe
he was different than other Chiricahuas. Maybe he
would harm Cynthia after all.

He'd never tell Hannah these thoughts.

And then there was his white name. Hector. Why
Hector? The noble son of Priam and Hecuba. The
champion of the Trojans who killed Patroclus in the
tenth year of the Trojan war only to be slain by the
great Achilles. Hector of Greek mythology had been

a breaker of wild horses who stood out in the battle-fields with his bright helmet. Hector the Apache wore a shimmering headband and definitely knew horseflesh. Homer had portrayed Hector as a man of great honor—hadn't the Trojans burned his body after nine days of mourning?—but Pete had always thought of Hector as the mortal enemy of all Greeks.

And if Hector the Apache touched one hair on Cynthia's head, Pete would do what Achilles did. He would slay the enemy.

Hannah didn't like the look of Marfa's posse. The man with the high derby hat who had caused Hannah to faint sat awkwardly in the saddle of some nag, passing a bottle labeled FRANKFORT RYE to the bearded cowboy he had been talking to at the depot when the train arrived with Geronimo. A couple of the Circle L waddies who had slipped liberal amounts of tanglefoot into the punch at the dance. A pale consumptive gambler who looked like he would be blown across the desert with the first gust of wind. The shotgun-toting town marshal. A grizzled Mexican vaquero with a glass eye, forking a fifty-year-old saddle and a paint horse about half that age. And pink-eyed, overweight Roland Jackson, Marfa's best cook.

Pete mounted Poseidon, his gray mustang that had proved time and again to be a stayer. Belissari wore tan ducking pants tucked into his Apache moccasins, a collarless white shirt with blue stripes, a red bandanna, and a battered slouch hat. A Remington revolver rested snug in a holster high on his right hip, and brass cartridges filled the shell belt. Two canteens had been fastened to his saddle horn over a lariat, with a linen duster strapped on top of his bedroll over the saddlebags behind the cantle. The scabbard on the right side sheathed a Winchester rifle.

At least Pete's prepared, Hannah thought as she pulled herself onto a buckskin gelding, *which is more that I can say for the rest of this sorry lot.*

"What's she doin' here?" the bearded cowboy said. Hannah could smell the whiskey on his breath.

"She's coming with us," the marshal said.

The bearded man spat. "She'll just slow us down, Bass. She ain't got no right—"

Hannah cut him off. "I've got more right than any one of you." With that, she kicked the buckskin into a trot and led the company out of town. Purple peaks stood towering in the distance to the east, south, and north, but they rode west into an endless sea of golden grass.

The leathery Indian cursed the palomino first in Spanish, then English, but Prancer refused to rise off the ground. They had ridden hard, Cynthia knew, and the mare had played out. Finally, the Apache spat and stormed a few yards away, looking east toward Marfa. Cynthia crawled to the horse, laced her fingers through the white mane, and mumbled an apology. Cynthia was hungry, bruised, tired, scared. She hadn't spoken to her captor at all, hadn't begged or cried—only screamed when he startled her at the livery—mainly because she didn't realize he understood English until this spate of profanity. A shadow crossed her face, and she looked into the empty black eyes.

Now she spoke, trying to sound calm, unafraid: "She'll be all right. You just rode her too hard, too long."

"Horses like it," he said.

"Anybody who tells you that horses like to be ridden is crazy," Pete told her more than once. *"At least, I've never met any horse like that."* Cynthia kept this to herself.

"What are you going to do?"

"You need a horse. We will use this one as bait. Don't worry. I will tie you up and set my trap away from here."

Chapter Four

*I*t takes an Apache to track an Apache.

Pete had heard that, or read it, maybe both. Now, as he studied the ground from his saddle, he realized how true the saying must be. He saw rocks and cheap grass, but nothing resembling a trail. And an Apache brave running from the Army and carrying a frightened ten-year-old girl had to leave some sign. Didn't he?

He nooned—though the sun told him noon had come and gone hours ago—on jerky and a few sips of tepid water from his canteen. Poseidon and the other mounts stood hobbled nearby, grazing in the wind. Marshal Bass—and especially Hannah—had wanted to push on, but Pete persuaded them to rest the horses. They hadn't pushed the animals. What was the point? They were basically just going in semicircles trying to find something they could follow, something they could guess was a mark left by Hector. But

28

Pete knew only fools would tire their horses when they might need them later.

That had been just one of the arguments that morning. "Them soldier boys seem to think Hector would take off for Mexico," Marshal Bass said. "How come we're headin' west?"

"I think Hector wants to go back to his homeland. That's west," Pete answered. "Besides, the Army patrol went south. We might as well go west. It's certain the Apache wouldn't go east or north. Too many people."

The man in the high derby snickered. "Best listen to him, Marshal. A man who dresses like an Apache is apt to think like one." High Derby seemed fairly in his cups by then. So was his friend Jim. Both men laughed. The rest of the posse ignored them.

"Wouldn't Mexico be safer?" Bass asked.

Pete shook his head. "Apaches hate Mexicans more than they hate Americans, or so I'm told. And it goes the other way, too."

The glass-eyed vaquero grinned wickedly and said, "*Sí,*" to confirm Pete's argument.

They continued west, cutting back and forth across the open spaces. Dismounting for a closer look at the earth. Looking for a piece of cloth, a broken blade of grass, a hoof print, or some depression.

Nothing.

By now, Pete thought maybe Marshal Bass had been right. Maybe Hector had ridden south to Mexico. Perhaps, he prayed, the soldiers had caught up with the Apache and were bringing Cynthia to Marfa at this very minute. It wasn't likely, though.

Pete corked the canteen and ripped off another bite of jerky.

Young and Collins, the two Circle L cowhands, stood watching the horses. Both men held Winchesters. For a while, the two friends had developed a severe case of nerves, half expecting Hector to ambush them at any moment. Now they merely looked bored. Snoring loudly, High Derby lay on the ground with his head against the saddle. At least now he had finally stopped complaining about the wind and sun. His bearded cowboy friend, Jim, sat nearby picking his teeth with a pocketknife. The two had quickly polished off their bottle of rye. The gambler, Artie Wilson, used a lone boulder for a backrest and sat cleaning his revolver, a Merwin & Hulbert .44-40 Pocket Army that looked like a British Bulldog. Across the camp, Marshal Bass chewed tobacco and nodded occasionally at whatever hung over Roland Jackson said. The ancient Mexican ignored everyone and honed the edge of his Bowie knife on a whetstone.

"What are you thinking?" Hannah asked.

Pete smiled. He answered in a whisper, "That we picked the wrong posse."

Hannah didn't reply. She didn't have to. Belissari knew she understood. They would be better off with the Army patrol. Most of those soldiers might be inexperienced, but the officer and sergeant knew what they were doing. Pete couldn't fault the men who joined Marfa's posse. They were willing to help, and he needed men. He only wished he had a better crew.

He recalled huddling with his sister and mother in their Corpus Christi home while their father read Homer to them by candlelight as a tropical cyclone pounded the Texas coast. Pete must have been ten or eleven at the time, and the captain read in Greek—Kostas Belissari had never learned English—while the frame house creaked and moaned in the wind. Odysseus and his men had run off the Cicons and sat feasting on the spoils of war. Odysseus wanted to leave immediately, but his men wouldn't listen. And then the Cicons returned with reinforcements, surprising and killing many Greeks before they escaped by the sea.

Pete had read Homer in Greek and English many times since then. Why think of that story now? He had no way of knowing that Cynthia, bound and gagged, lay thinking about Homer, too, remembering a story Pete had read to her and the others during a thunderstorm. She tried to recall the prayer Odysseus had said in *The Odyssey. "Oh, Zeus!"*—she couldn't remember the middle part—*"Please return me home!"*

Swallowing the last bit of jerky, Pete rose and pressed his hand against the Remington's butt. A sudden coldness had made his skin crawl.

"What's the matter?" Hannah asked, concern etched in her face.

"Probably nothing," he said, and walked toward the horses. The chill persisted. He felt a sudden fear that Hector would lead an army of Cicons against the posse and drive them back to Marfa or to Hades itself.

"These horses have rested long enough," he said. "Let's get moving."

Before Pete could take another step, Poseidon's ears pricked forward and the mustang lifted its head and looked up toward the small rise directly behind him. Belissari spun around . . . and held his breath.

The palomino mare stolen from Clay Evans's livery stood chewing on cheap grass, swatting flies with her tail but otherwise not moving.

"Young!" Pete called out. "You and Collins gather those horses. Bring them into camp." He turned to the black-bearded cowboy. "You help them."

The man called Jim snarled, "Since when do you give orders?"

Marshal Bass yelled, "Do it!" The cowboy folded his knife, grabbed his lariat, and walked toward the grazing animals. Pete took a few steps across the camp until he stood beside the Marfa lawman and cook, staring at the palomino. Hannah followed him. So did the Mexican and gambler.

Five minutes passed in silence.

"Well?" Bass asked.

"It means we've got him!" Roland Jackson blurted out. "That Apache's on foot now. We'll run that sucker down and make him remember the Alamo!"

Hannah didn't understand the Alamo reference. She assumed that the cook still hadn't sobered up.

"No," the Mexican answered. "The horse is a trap. Any man who goes to get the animal will be killed by the Apache."

Pete nodded. "I think he's right. That mare isn't moving. My guess is she's hobbled."

"Probably lame," the Mexican said. "The Apache needs another horse."

Hannah spun around. She saw the two Circle L

cowboys leading in a few horses, including Poseidon and her horse. She counted. Two . . . three . . . four . . . five . . . six . . . seven. High Derby's friend pulled the three other mounts behind him. She sighed, and blinked. And then—

"Look out!" she screamed.

Hector appeared out of nowhere, as if he had sprouted from the grass. The Indian swung a stick—ax? Hannah couldn't tell—as the belligerent cowboy Jim turned. Even at this distance, she heard the sickening *thunk* as the cowhand collapsed. The Circle L boys ran, pulling the horses as fast as they could, toward camp. They had exchanged their rifles for ropes when they went to round up the horses. Pete charged past Hannah to his own saddle, and pulled the Winchester from the scabbard.

On the prairie, Hector had thrown Jim over one of the horses, then leaped onto the back of the lead mount and let out a terrifying war whoop. The three animals galloped toward the west.

Pete jacked the lever of the Winchester and brought the stock to his right shoulder. Hannah held her breath, bit her lower lip, and watched as the rifle barrel made a line across the sky as Pete aimed.

The Winchester boomed. Hannah blinked from the acrid smoke. She looked.

Hector had stopped, but remained mounted. He lifted whatever it was that he had clubbed Jim with high over his head and shouted something. They didn't know if Jim was dead or alive.

"Besdacada!" carried with the wind.

"Again!" Bass yelled. "Shoot again. Now, while he's not movin'."

Pete had already cocked the rifle. He held the Winchester steady, let out a slight breath, and squeezed the trigger. Hannah's ears rang from the explosion. She squinted. Hector hadn't fallen.

The marshal swore. "How could you miss that shot?" he shouted. By now the vaquero had found his own rifle, a long-range single-shot Remington Rolling Block. He slammed the stock against his shoulder and pulled the trigger just as Hector took off at a high lope.

He, too, missed.

Pete fired again, and the gambler emptied his revolver—though the Indian was well out of pistol range—as Hector and the three horses disappeared over the rise.

"Get those horses saddled!" Bass snapped as the cowboys brought in the animals.

In the excitement, Hannah tried to calm herself. Hector had gotten away with three horses, but they were on his trail. And he was close. At least he didn't have a rifle. But where was Cynthia? She threw the saddle blanket on her horse and said a prayer for Jim, even though she hadn't liked him or his friend. She stopped in mid-thought, and turned. High Derby?

"Where's the other man?"

The cowboy named Collins, closest to her, looked at the spot where the man had been sleeping and swore. "Jim said he woke up right before y'all spotted that mare."

Hannah's gaze fell upon High Derby's saddle. He had taken his rifle with him.

A gunshot cut through the air. The bay horse Artie Wilson was saddling let out a chilling cry, reared, and collapsed, kicking and screaming as another shot dropped Roland Jackson's mule without a sound.

At the smell of blood, Hannah's horse pulled away, burning her fingers with the reins, and took off at a high lope toward Marfa. She fell to her knees, shaking both hands to fight the burning pain, and cringed as another horse dropped. A bullet whined off a nearby rock.

"Get down!" someone yelled.

Another voice: "Get them horses on the ground!"

Hannah flattened herself against the ground. She looked up. Pete had forced Poseidon to lie on the ground. "Easy, boy," he kept saying as the mustang tried to rise. Collins had also managed to get his horse to the safety of the ground, but the marshal's mount had broken its reins and sprinted after Hannah's terrified horse. They had only two horses, and they were pinned down.

Darkness came welcomed. Pete staked Poseidon and Collins's buckskin in a natural depression, and posted the two Circle L cowboys as guards. Roland Jackson wanted a fire, but Marshal Bass lambasted him and said he wasn't giving that devil Hector anything to shoot at.

"That Apache probably took off before dark," the cook argued. "We ain't heard from him in hours."

"You want to go on a scout, check things out, make sure, you go right ahead, fatso," Bass snapped.

Jackson looked taken aback. "You got no right to

call me that, Amos. It ain't my fault we're in this fix. It's his." His fat finger pointed straight at Pete. "He missed. I coulda knocked that savage off his horse with that shot."

Pete said nothing. Jackson was right. Belissari still didn't understand how he had missed. The first shot? Sure. Hector was on a fast horse a couple of hundred yards away. The wind. The elevation. Pete considered himself a good shot, but far from a sharpshooter. That had been a tough shot. But the second one? He hadn't flinched. He had accounted for the wind. He had drawn a bead on the Apache's chest. What had happened?

Surprisingly, the vaquero took up for Belissari. "I, too, missed, hombre," he told the cook. "And I had a rifle with much longer range than the repeater of the caballero." The old-timer smiled. "And I have much more experience shooting Apaches than Señor Belissari."

The Mexican had even pronounced Pete's name right.

"So how did you miss?" Jackson asked.

The man shrugged. "It was like this. This Apache buck has a protector. Do not laugh. It is true. A god came down from the sky and plucked my bullet out of the air. This god did the same thing when Señor Belissari fired."

Roland Jackson scoffed.

Pete Belissari, however, wasn't quite so sure that the vaquero had been joking.

Chapter Five

The high-pitched howls of coyotes woke Hannah from a restless sleep. She sat up and waited for her eyes to adjust to darkness. Her skin crawled at the sound of the predators, unlike any of the yips or cries she had ever heard from an animal. Hannah stiffened. Those screams didn't come from a coyote, or a wolf.

"Pete?" she called out.

No answer.

Hannah stood in a panic. "Pete!"

She heard again the raw, agonizing scream amplified by a cloudy night sky. Hannah felt pulled to the noise, and she found herself walking out of camp when a hand fell hard on her shoulder and pulled her back. "Easy, miss," the gambler, Artie Wilson, said.

"Where's Pete?"

"He went out on a scout about an hour ago."

Another scream. Hannah shivered.

"That ain't your beau, ma'am. My guess is it's them two drunks we brung along."

"Why?"

Another voice answered, "The Apache who is called Hector will keep those two fools alive as long as he so desires." It was the vaquero, the one Hannah disliked most of all. "He draws power by torturing them." Another scream. "Listen. They already scream for death." The Mexican laughed. "He is good, this Hector. I will enjoy taking revenge on the last bronco Apache."

"You're pathetic," Hannah said.

"*Sí,*" he answered, and laughed again as another shriek wailed with the night wind.

Footsteps sounded. Hannah made out two forms to her right and smelled the whiskey on Roland Jackson's breath before he even spoke. "I don't like this a'tall," he said. Marshal Bass told the old cook to put a sock in it.

"How long you reckon he'll keep it up?" Bass asked to no one in particular.

"All night," the gambler replied. "Make us edgy, keep us from sleeping."

Jackson grunted something. Marshal Bass swore. Outside of camp, suddenly, came a new voice: "Hello in camp. It's Pete. I'm coming in."

Hannah sighed, but her relief was short-lived. A rifled cocked and boomed. The muzzle flash blinded her. The gunshot was deafening. "It's a trick!" Jackson screamed, and fired four more rounds before someone knocked him senseless.

"You fool!" Bass snapped.

Hannah swallowed. She couldn't speak. "Belissari!" the gambler called out. "You all right?"

A loud burst of profanity made Hannah smile.

Pete Belissari hobbled into camp, barely able to stand on his right leg. He used his Winchester for a crutch, felt Hannah at his side, and finally sank onto the ground. His right foot throbbed. He tested it gingerly, shaking his head. A match flared. Artie Wilson held it over the horseman's leg.

"You hit?" Marshal Bass asked.

"No," Pete answered. "I smashed my foot against a rock diving for cover."

Belissari looked at the faces staring at him. Roland Jackson couldn't meet his stare. "What were you thinking?"

"Well, I, uh . . . it . . . you-you shouldn't have snuck up on us like that, Pete."

Pete swore again. "I said, 'Hello in camp. It's Pete. I'm coming in.' What did you want me to say: 'It's Hector. Prepare to die'?" He shook his head, and cringed as Hannah tried to pull off his moccasin.

Wilson lighted another match.

"I don't think that match is a good idea," the drunken cook said, but no one listened to him.

Hannah pulled off a sock. The foot was scarred where a large piece of glass had speared him during a fight on top of a train earlier in the year. That wound had healed over pretty well, at least. Hannah shook her head. Pete suppressed a groan, leaned forward, and pulled on his sock. It hurt like blazes. Next he took the moccasin from Hannah and slowly, painfully, managed to put it back on and tighten the rawhide thongs over his calf and foot. Hannah's eyes told him what he already knew: The foot was broken. How badly, he wasn't sure, but he wouldn't be running any races any time soon.

Artie shook out the match before it burned his fingers. He didn't light another one.

"You think you'll be able to ride?" the gambler asked.

"It's my right foot," he said. "I won't have to put any weight on it when I mount. I'll be fine on horseback."

Roland Jackson managed to slur out, "You should wear boots."

The screams of High Derby and Jim stopped shortly before dawn. Hannah didn't know if that meant the two were dead, or what. The palomino mare remained where they had first spotted it yesterday. It had to be hobbled. But there was no sign of Hector, or Cynthia. As the sun crept above the horizon, the men gathered at the center of camp. Roland Jackson complained that they had no choice but to return to Marfa. After all, they only had two horses and couldn't track down Hector on foot. Jackson said they should leave now, before the Apache started to pick them off one by one. Nobody paid much attention to the cook. One of the cowboys pointed out that perhaps Cal Evans's palomino could be ridden. "Who wants to go fetch her?" Jackson said. No one answered. But with two horses or three, Hannah knew the cook was right: The posse had been stopped.

"We have nothing to fear from Hector," the vaquero

said. "He pulled out during the night, taking the girl with him."

"How do you know that?" Hannah asked.

The Mexican shrugged. "He has no reason to stay. We cannot pursue. He would not wait to kill us, knowing the Army is after him. He is long gone."

"Then let's get the Sam Hill out of here!" Jackson blurted out.

"What about those two men?" Hannah asked.

"They're dead," the cook said. "Let's go. Now!"

Pete pulled himself up and, using the Winchester as a crutch, hobbled out of camp. Hannah followed him. So did the vaquero and one of the cowboys. They stopped beside the mare, and the cowboy removed the hobbles on her forefeet. "Why don't you take her down with the other horses?" Pete suggested. "Check her out. See if she's lame, or if we can saddle her up." The cowboy nodded. Pete led the way from camp.

Fifteen minutes later, they found High Derby and Jim.

Hannah turned away from the horrible sight. She fell onto her knees, overcome with nausea.

The glass-eyed Mexican smiled. "Hector did not cut off their heads. He is getting soft."

Belissari fought off a wave of nausea and cut the rawhide bonds that held the two men over the hot coals. Pete then turned from the ghastly sight. The vaquero laughed, not offering to help, but Pete ignored his callousness and turned back toward High Derby and Jim.

"They're alive," Pete said. "Somehow."

"Put them out of their misery, señor," the Mexican said.

"No." This came from Hannah. She shoved the old scalphunter aside and knelt beside Pete. "Bring some blankets and water. Some whiskey if that old sot Jackson hasn't drunk it all." She turned back toward the vaquero. "Now!"

When he was gone, Hannah looked at Pete. "I don't even know where to start." One of the men reached out and gripped Hannah's right hand. His voice croaked out a barely audible, "Help me." Hannah couldn't tell if the man was High Derby or Jim.

Pete rose. "I'll send Collins back on his horse to fetch a doctor and a wagon to take these two back to Marfa." Hannah nodded. As Pete limped back toward camp, she patted the man's burned hand softly and told him everything would be all right.

Hector had pulled the shoes off the palomino's hind hooves, just to make sure the mare couldn't be ridden. Pete mounted Poseidon and circled the camp for a couple of miles, making sure that the Apache had left. Satisfied, he rode east and tracked down Hannah's runaway horse. That took him a couple of hours, and it was high noon when he returned to the camp. The cavalry patrol was there when he got back. Sgt. Quincannon greeted him with a handshake and steaming cup of black coffee.

"Y'all ran head-on into misfortune," the soldier said.

Pete nodded. He started to take a sip of coffee, but the liquid burned his lips so he let it cool. Lt. Hammond approached the two men, wiping his sweaty brow, and held out a gauntleted hand. Pete shifted the coffee cup to his left hand and shook the officer's hand. "Sorry you ran into Hector and not us," the officer said, not boastfully. "I've sent a galloper to Fort Davis to bring medical supplies and personnel to Marfa for those two tortured men." He shook his head and cursed the Apache's handiwork.

"I see you found a horse."

Pete nodded. The officer placed his hands on his hips and looked west. "I plan to leave one man here with the wounded. We'll take his horse. That means three of your posse can come with us. You men probably know this land better than any of us. We'll hire you on as civilian scouts. It pays a dollar a day."

"You can keep your money, Lieutenant," Pete said, "as far as I'm concerned. I'll go with you."

Both soldiers had noticed Pete favoring his injured foot. "You sure you're up to it, sir?" Quincannon asked. "We'll be riding hard after that rascal. You should stay here and receive medical attention."

"My foot can wait," Pete said. "I'm going on."

"So am I," said Hannah, who had just walked up. Before the officer could argue, she launched into a tirade that he could not, would not, stop her. Hammond simply nodded.

"We can take one more," the lieutenant said. "If anyone else wishes to come along."

Marshal Bass and Roland Jackson stared at the ground. The cowboy shuffled his feet and mumbled something unintelligible. Artie Wilson shot a glance at the vaquero. The scalphunter rose, smiling, and said,

"I am that third man, señors. I know the Apaches better than anyone. You will need me before this is over."

The gambler accepted that with a slight nod. Pete wished Artie Wilson, and not the glass-eyed Mexican, had put up a fight, but he couldn't blame him. He could tell that Hannah disliked the scalphunter. Pete didn't care much for the old man himself. He admittedly had killed Apaches—men, women, and children—for a reward from the Mexican government, a policy that condoned wanton murder. The only reason the Mexican wanted to come along was the opportunity to butcher people one more time.

But they were stuck with him. For now.

"All right," Lt. Hammond said. "Mount up." He looked at Marshal Bass. "I hate to leave you like this, Marshal, before I know for certain that you have help for your wounded, but I don't want to give Hector any more of a head start."

"I understand," Bass said. "Good luck to you."

Pete pulled himself into the saddle, swinging his right foot high over the cantle and bedroll and easing it into the stirrup. He would kick free of the stirrup when he could to ease the pain. They rode out in the heat of the day, moving west. The Mexican took off ahead of the others to look for signs, although Pete had little confidence in Hector ever leaving anything for them to find. Sgt. Quincannon pulled up beside Belissari.

"I might as well let you know now," the sergeant said, "that our orders are to proceed only as far as Fort Selden in New Mexico Territory, or until we capture or kill Hector."

Pete understood. "We appreciate your help, Sergeant. We'll go on with another patrol at Fort Selden if need be."

Quincannon cleared his throat, and shifted uncomfortably in the McClellan saddle. "Mr. Belissari, I doubt if there will be another patrol if we don't catch Hector before we reach New Mexico," he said in a whisper. "Now I wouldn't speak of this to Miss Scott, but Lt. Hammond thinks Hector has probably killed the girl and will disappear into Mexico. And I'll deny ever saying this, but, sir, well, you know it's true. You've lived out here. The only way the Army was ever able to track down Geronimo was because of the Apache scouts. And we've sent all the scouts to Florida with the hostiles. This patrol, or any patrol for that matter, won't be able to find Hector unless he wants to be found."

Quincannon shook his head and spit. "No, sir, I don't think we'll ever find that Indian or that girl."

Chapter Six

Hannah and Pete learned the name of the vaquero in La Mesilla. The three had entered the New Mexico village after leaving Hammond, Quincannon, and the other soldiers at Fort Selden. Quincannon had been right. The Army decided that Hector had escaped into Mexico; he certainly hadn't been seen north of the border. "With deepest apologies, Miss Scott," the commanding officer at Fort Selden had said, "I fear the United States Army has done everything it has been able to do in this matter. My only suggestion would be for you to contact Mexican authorities, or continue this search on your own. I'm sorry."

The scalphunter said he would be glad to continue on with Hannah and the horseman. It gave him pleasure. Perhaps the gringo *soldados* were right. Maybe old Hector had dipped across the border and aimed to take young Cynthia to the Sierra Madres or another ancient Apache stronghold. Either way, the vaquero said, Pete and Hannah needed him. He could track down Hector. He knew Apaches.

So they turned south toward La Mesilla, the desert floor shimmering as they approached the cottonwoods along the Rio Grande. The Mexican walked. He had to leave his borrowed cavalry mount at the fort. They needed to buy a horse for the scalphunter and supplies, a pack animal, maybe find some men willing to ride after Hector, with luck a better posse than they had found in Marfa. And Pete needed to have a doctor look at his black-and-blue right foot.

As Pete and Hannah tied their horses to a hitching post in front of a hotel on the plaza, a young voice cried out: *"¡Ayudame! Es el diablo, el asasino de su propia gente."* Pete turned. The vaquero, eyes blazing, spun around, pushed Belissari over the hitching rail, and snatched Poseidon's reins. Before Pete could untangle his feet from the cedar post, the Mexican had pulled a flying mount into the saddle and had the gray mustang at a gallop raising dust across the plaza. Horse and rider disappeared around the corner of one of the old adobe buildings. Hannah helped Belissari to his feet. They heard a gunshot. Somebody screamed. Hooves pounded on sun-baked bricks.

The vaquero wheeled around the building, followed by several Mexican men and a few women. One of the men raised an old musket. More concerned with the chances of his horse getting shot than the scalphunter, Pete somehow managed to pull himself onto the top of the cedar hitching post. He used an adobe column for support, timed his jump, and leaped as Poseidon sped by. Belissari wrapped his arms around the

Mexican's waist. A hoof clipped his broken foot. The old man flattened his nose with a rock-like palm. Pete felt himself sailing. He saw the blueness of the sky, the brownness of the dirt, and then a flash of orange, red, yellow, and black as pain wracked his head and the breath left his lungs.

When he could breathe again, he remembered that his foot hurt. Blood poured from his nose.

A gunshot brought him to his senses. As his vision cleared, he realized the Mexican and Poseidon still lived, uninjured. Someone swore in Spanish, then English. The mustang slid to a stop, finding another path blocked, and took off west. A giant Mexican in white cotton ran out of a cantina, never slowing down, and leaped into the air, tackling the vaquero and sending both to the ground in a cloud of dust. That's what Pete had meant to do. He had just failed miserably. Two other men managed to stop Poseidon. Belissari let out a sigh. His horse was all right.

People screamed with excitement, and the glass-eyed Mexican and his assailant disappeared as a crowd circled them. Hannah helped Pete to his feet. He unloosened his bandanna and held it against his bloody nose and limped across the plaza. They had the vaquero disarmed, and pretty much bloodied, by the time they could push their way through the crowd.

A man wearing a black Boss of the Plains Stetson and gray frock coat, with a five-point star pinned to the lapel, grabbed the Mexican's throat and studied the malevolent face. "Well, well, well," the lawman said in a Texas accent. "Emilio Vasquez. I've been waitin' to hang you for five years."

* * *

In the spring of 1881, Emilio Vasquez led his gang of vicious scalphunters against a group of freighters in the Burro Mountains southwest of Deming. Only an eight-year-old boy survived, hiding behind a dead ox and watching in horror as Vasquez, easily recognized by his ugly face and glass eye, and his men killed the freighters and their families.

Hannah shook her head when the marshal finished the story.

"Murderin' Mexican freighters is a lot easier than killin' bronco Apaches," the lawman said. "I warrant those weren't the first Mexicans Vasquez butchered. We're lucky the boy recognized him. He's been livin' here with an aunt since the massacre. Y'all should be a little more careful 'bout the company you keep. He wants to see you, though." The marshal nodded at Pete.

Belissari turned to Hannah. They decided that she would buy a packhorse at the livery and some supplies at the mercantile, while Pete would see what Vasquez wanted and then find a doctor. No one had seen any signs of Hector in Mesilla, so they would head west, stopping at Deming and Lordsburg before crossing into Arizona Territory and interviewing the commanding officer at Fort Bowie. If Hector hadn't been seen by then, they would head into Mexico.

Pete found Vasquez on a narrow cot in the dark, damp adobe dungeon, his hands handcuffed in front of him and his left ankle chained to an anvil. The marshal took no chances with this man. Belissari couldn't blame him. The vaquero sat up. "I am sorry to have broken your nose, señor, but, as you see, I am not popular in this village."

Belissari opted to remain silent. What did the old scalphunter want? Maybe he would suggest where they might find Hector and Cynthia. He had no chance of escape. Maybe he would do something decent in his life before he died. Vasquez grinned, and Pete knew that had been wishful thinking.

"You must get me out of this jail, Belissari," the Mexican said in a hoarse voice. "Then we will be able to kill this fiend of an Apache and rescue your little girl. It is the only way."

Pete shook his head. "What chance would we have tracking Hector while dodging a posse?"

Vasquez stood and leaned against the metal bars on the door. He glanced toward the marshal's office upstairs, and, satisfied that he and Pete were alone, whispered, "Posses can be lost, amigo. This close to Mexico, they would think we would cross the border. And we would. But then we could double back. Hector is not in Mexico. He will join his father, the great warrior Matitzal. This is the truth, señor."

He had Pete's attention. Matitzal? Belissari had never heard the name. Pete studied the scalphunter's face, his cold eye. Could the old man be lying? Was this a bluff to get out of a hangman's noose? Belissari couldn't tell.

"How do you know this?"

The vaquero laughed. "I have told you many times that I know the Apache. Matitzal is of great interest to me, more than his son. It was Matitzal who murdered my parents in 1846. For forty years, I have vowed to kill him. Now you must break me out of this jail, señor, and we will find those Apache butchers and have our revenge."

"How do you know they aren't in Mexico?"

Vasquez turned and sat down on the bunk without answering.

Pete thought for a minute. The marshal had no deputy. He wouldn't expect anything. They were almost spitting distance from Mexico. Escape would be easy. Vasquez was right. Cross the border, double back. . . . He thought about Hannah and Cynthia. The Mexican government's policy of paying a bounty for dead Apaches angered him anyway. But Vasquez sickened him even more. He would be trusting this killer with their lives, this butcher who murdered his own people.

"Vasquez," he said icily, "I've never made a pact with the devil, and I don't intend to start now."

The scalphunter leaped from his bunk and gripped the bars again, his face a mask of fury. "Hear me out, Belissari. You get me out of this stinkhole or I will kill you, and that pretty Hannah, too. Emilio Vasquez keeps his word."

Pete restrained from spitting in the Mexican's face. "You'll have a hard time doing that," he said, stepping away from the jail cell. "You're going to hang, Vasquez, after a trial—if they have a trial."

He walked up the steps, ignoring the scalphunter's threats and vile curses.

JACK LESLIE, M.D. Pete stared at the shingle before gingerly dismounting. He had known a Dr. Jack Leslie in Texas, a captain with the Tenth Cavalry who had retired a year or so back shortly after the regiment moved to Arizona Territory. Could it be the same man? Pete wondered as he entered the office. In a way, he hoped so. Then again, as he recalled the good doctor's manners . . .

Doc Leslie smiled as he got Pete on the table, cut away the leather moccasin, and yanked off a dirty sock, causing Belissari to bite his lip. "That's a pretty color of black and purple," Leslie said as he held out the injured foot. "Interesting scar, too. Pete, my boy, you are the most accident-prone young man I've ever met. If I had hung my shingle in Fort Davis instead of La Mesilla, I'd be rich now. Let's see, this little piggy—"

Belissari yelled. Jack Leslie laughed.

"Want me to set that busted nose of yours while I'm at it?" Leslie asked.

"No," Pete said, but the doctor reached over and did it anyway.

Pete swore underneath his breath, tested his aching nose, studied Jack Leslie's wicked grin, and regretted ever setting foot in this office.

"I could amputate that foot of yours," Leslie said. "But I imagine you'd prefer I didn't, right?"

"I . . ." Pete decided not to answer.

"Amputation's cheaper."

Belissari kept quiet. Leslie laughed. "Four toes are broken, and some of the bones in the foot. It's swollen a lot, but if you've ridden all the way from Texas like that, I don't see any reason why you can't keep on. I'll wrap it up, and give you a pair of boots. That should be a little more comfortable. Besides, you need something new since I cut your moccasin off. I think I've got just what you need. Sit up, boy. I'm done with you except for the foot wrapping."

Pete obeyed and watched Leslie pull back a white sheet on another table and pull a pair of black cavalry boots off a corpse. He held the sole of the boot against Belissari's foot, nodded, and gave the boots to Pete. "Yes, sir, these should do," the doctor commented as he began wrapping the badly bruised foot.

Belissari swallowed and looked first at the boots, then at the corpse's socks.

"Don't fret, Petros, that old boy won't be needing any footwear where he's going."

"How did he die?"

"Cholera."

Pete swore and threw the boots across the room, wiping his hands on the sheets. Jack Leslie cackled. "Pete, you are not only accident-prone, you're gullible. That soldier boy got drunk, picked a fight with the wrong fellow, and got hisself killed." Still laughing, Leslie finished bandaging the foot, walked across the office, and returned with the black boots.

"Put them on," the doctor ordered.

Belissari cringed as the right boot went on. He eased himself to the floor and walked to the wall and back, still limping, but feeling a bit better. The boots were probably a size too big, but that didn't matter. He could ride in them. He felt better.

"Doc," Pete said, "you ever heard of an Apache named Matitzal?"

"Matitzal? Why, yes I have. He was one of Mangas Coloradas's lieutenants. Scalphunters or Mexican soldiers, I can't remember which, ambushed him down in Sonora during the War of the Rebellion. I guess he's been dead for more than twenty years. Why do you ask?"

Pete said it didn't matter. Emilio Vasquez had been lying. Belissari thanked the doctor and headed for the door.

"Just a minute," Leslie called out. "That'll be ten dollars."

"Ten dollars! That's robbery, Doc."

Jack Leslie smiled. "I told you amputation's cheaper."

Chapter Seven

Fort Bowie, Arizona Territory, sprawled beneath the chaparral on the high desert mountains. Hannah hadn't expected to receive any good news at the sprawling post, so she couldn't say she felt disappointed when an Irish captain told her Hector had not been spotted in Mexico or the United States. "Maybe he's dead," the officer said, and immediately regretted the words. If the Apache was dead, chances were Cynthia was, too. She couldn't survive alone, lost in the harsh wilderness.

Pete and Hannah rode out silently, past the abandoned Indian agency and post cemetery, through Apache Pass, and stopped at the stone stagecoach station to water their horses. The November afternoon had turned warm, so Hannah found some shade underneath a massive Arizona walnut tree. She dipped hardtack in bitter coffee to soften the hardened food. No wonder so many soldiers had broken teeth. A horse snorted, and Hannah turned to see Pete leading their horses and pack mule. She had expected to be at the old Butterfield station at least an hour, maybe longer.

"Feel like riding to Lordsburg?" he asked.

Actually, she would have preferred to take the stage there. Sitting in a saddle—what had it been, six weeks?—had left her stiff, sunburned, dirty, and sore. Lordsburg lay in New Mexico, between the Pyramid and Burro mountains. They had been there maybe a week ago.

"Why?" she asked.

"Station master told me a story. Seems a passenger the day before yesterday said his brother owns a ranch just north of Lordsburg. Someone stole a couple of his horses, but left three worn-out mounts behind. One of them had a Circle L brand."

Hannah splashed the rest of her coffee against a prickly pear, spit out the unsoftened hardtack, and swung into the saddle, forgetting about her aching muscles. One of the horses Hector had stolen back in Texas had been a Circle L gelding.

"I do not mind the trade—the three horses these two left behind are fine animals, just need rest and good grain—but Juan Auza would like to have a say in the matter," Juan Auza said. "It was just luck that I checked the pasture where I was keeping those horses. I saw the bay and said to myself, 'Juan Auza, that is not your horse.' Next I found the other two animals and said to myself, 'Juan Auza, something is wrong here.' I rode around and found two of my horses missing. You say you are trailing these two takers of horses?"

Pete said they were but before he could ask another question, Hannah blurted out, "You say two people?"

"*Sí,* señorita. Juan Auza is not blind. He can read sign. One of these men was a man of your size." He nodded at Pete. "The other was a young boy. I—"

"Could the young one have been a girl?" Hannah asked.

Juan shrugged. "*Sí.* I did not consider that possibility. So who is this man and girl who take the fine horses of Juan Auza without his permission?"

Pete wondered if Juan Auza, who spoke of himself in the third person, would think him crazy for telling him the horse thief was an Apache. But he told him anyway. The rancher simply nodded, unfazed by the answer. Belissari took off his hat and ran his fingers through his hair. Hector had gotten careless—finally.

"Did you follow them?" Hannah asked.

"*Sí,* but I lost the trail that evening. They were headed north, though, perhaps trying to catch up with the other Apaches."

Belissari almost dropped his hat. "What other Apaches?"

"I saw the sign of an Apache camp near Skeleton Canyon a month or so ago. And the husband of my oldest sister, who lives near Silver City, said he saw several Apaches heading northwest a short while later. He told the sheriff, but the husband of my sister had been drinking much tequila at the time and the sheriff did not believe him. Nor did anyone believe Juan

Auza. But I know what I saw, and I believe the husband of my sister."

Pete thanked the rancher and turned to go.

"If you catch up with this thief, tell him Juan Auza is not angry," said the rancher, either unconcerned or unaware that the Circle L Ranch and Cal Evans's Livery might want their stolen horses returned to them. "I will keep the horses he left me and call it a fair trade. The brother of my eldest sister said it looked like the Apaches were going to Hades. If you wish to find them, you might have to go to Hades yourself."

Hades, New Mexico Territory, rested in the Mogollon Mountains, a hard climb on horseback on something that passed for a road as long as it didn't rain or snow. Six years earlier, Hades had been nothing but boulders, elk, and evergreen, but a sergeant stationed at Fort Bayard stuck his supper plate in Silver Creek just to pass the time and found color. When his enlistment was up, he staked a claim, produced gold and silver, and pretty soon had plenty of company. The sergeant sold out in 1884, retired to San Francisco, and left Hades to, well, his less-refined neighbors.

Civilization had come to most of New Mexico. Railroads carried travelers to Santa Fe or Deming or across the territory toward California or Missouri. The violent Lincoln County War had been relegated to songs, big windies, and Pat Garrett's book about Billy the Kid. But Hades, though a young town, had become a throwback to the halcyon days of old. In this year alone, the *Santa Fe New Mexican* reported, there had been seven reported murders, including the shooting of the latest town marshal. No one in Hades had bothered to keep a running tally on the number of robberies, assaults, and other crimes.

It was no place for a lady.

Hannah argued anyway, but Pete finally persuaded her to stay at a shack north of the mining town. It didn't take two people to ask a few questions and pick up some beans and coffee. Besides, the clouds threatened rain, so Hannah might as well stay at the shack and keep an eye on her horse and the mule. The storm blew in at dusk, a couple of hours after Belissari left, and Hannah suspected that Pete had gotten the better end of the bargain.

" 'No need for us both to get wet,' he says," she commented to the small fire in front of her as water poured off the brim of her hat and down her India rubber poncho. "Shack" wasn't so accurate a description of the place they had picked to camp. Pine logs had been felled and stacked into a C-shaped structure about four feet high. An old wagon tarp, more sieve than solid, served as a roof, but some miner had once called this home. Now Hannah sat with the rats, wondering how long the fire would last.

Her horse whinnied. The mule stamped its feet in the mud. Hannah looked up. It was too soon for Pete. She reached under the poncho and drew the Remington revolver he had left her. Ducking to avoid the soaked canvas roof, she moved to the edge of the shack as the rats scurried for cover. Hannah blinked. The two animals stood hobbled in a stand of pines, alert, nervous. Something was out there. Bear? Panther? Wolf? Man?

Hannah thumbed back the hammer and stepped into the cold, driving rain. The animals studied her with interest as she approached them. She patted the mule's neck with her left hand and looked around but saw only the blackness of the forest. Thunder rolled. Something popped behind her, and she spun around, slipping on the wet ground, and almost shot herself in the leg. A small limb, broken by the wind, bounced down a swaying tree and fell to the ground.

She sighed, scrambled to her feet, and was about to head to the makeshift shelter when she spotted the leather pouch beside a pine cone. Hannah shifted the Remington to her left hand and snatched the pouch. She recognized the design: Apache. An amulet, said to carry a warrior's medicine. Hannah lowered the hammer and balanced the revolver on her thigh and worked at the rawhide drawstring on the pouch, opened it, and dumped the contents onto the ground. Two beads, the spent brass cartridge of a large caliber rifle, an eagle's talon, and a human tooth. A child's tooth.

"Cynthia." Hannah gasped.

She felt the presence behind her, knew she had been duped, and shot to her feet, jerking the revolver. A vise tightened against her right wrist and the Remington spun away. She felt herself being twisted. Someone tried to jerk her arm out of the socket. Another hand grasped her hair and pulled her head back, and then she was slammed forward into the ground. She sucked in air, rain, and grass, trying to reach out for the revolver. A foot slammed into her ribs and she rolled onto her back, groaning. Air left her lungs.

She felt her assailant's fists clench her wrists and pin her arms to the ground. Tears and rain streamed down her cheek. Hannah stared up at Hector. His eyes no longer looked so gentle.

The man at the livery said yes, he had heard a few stories about people seeing a party of Apache making its way toward the San Francisco Mountains, but he put no stock in them. People, he said, had also seen Billy the Kid, John Wilkes Booth, Jesse James, and Abe Lincoln wandering around as bold as brass after their reported deaths. The last band of hostile Apaches was on its way to Florida.

Belissari thanked him and rode down Front Street before hitching Poseidon in front of the general store next to a burned-out alley. Quick trips into one of many saloons, the only reputable-looking hotel, and the land office resulted in one beer, two strange looks, and no information. Hades had been a long shot, so he decided to go back to Hannah after buying the coffee and beans. When he came out of the store, two men stood admiring Poseidon. Pete hesitated for a second, wishing he had not given Hannah his revolver. Then he decided otherwise. Those two men probably would have taken the Remington from him and fed it to him.

One stood about six-foot-four with a chest the size of a rain barrel and a face that looked as if it had caught fire once and had been put out with an ax. He wore greasy buckskins, a hat from the days of the

Mexican War, and a belt around his waist that held two revolvers, a skinning knife, and a Bowie the size of a small sword.

The second man, obviously a brother, stood at least two inches taller, but had three fewer fingers and one less ear. He carried a long shotgun in his right hand—the one missing only the little finger—and warmed his other hand—the one without the thumb and forefinger—on the hilt of a Green River knife. It was this man who spotted Pete and smiled.

It started to rain.

"This your horse, mister?" Big Ugly Senior asked.

Belissari nodded and strapped his supplies behind the cantle.

"Nice mustang," Big Ugly Junior said.

Pete thanked the man, ducked under Poseidon, and reached for the reins.

"You'd be Pete Belissari?" one of the men said.

Pete turned. He hadn't given his name to anyone in town. Nobody knew he was in Hades, except Hannah and Juan Auza. Big Ugly Junior shifted the shotgun into his left hand and continued. "Lookin' for an Apache who took off with your little girl?"

"That's right," Pete said, suddenly interested in the two brutes.

The leviathans laughed. "Our pard wants to see you."

Belissari shifted uncomfortably. The two men looked past him. Slowly, Pete looked into the charred alley. He didn't make a try for the sheathed Winchester. Instead, he sighed and felt the muzzles of the shotgun against his spine.

"Amigo." Emilio Vasquez's good eye beamed. "Alas, I did not hang in La Mesilla, bless the good marshal's soul. Do you remember the sods from Marfa that Hector caught?" He didn't wait for Pete to answer. "What they went through will be nothing, my friend, compared with what I have planned for you. I told you I would kill you and I shall. But first, tell me: Where is that firebrand, Miss Scott?"

Pete didn't answer. The Ugly brothers shoved him into the alley.

"You will tell me," Vasquez said. "You will scream out all you know."

Chapter Eight

Every step the horse took jarred Hannah's ribs. Her neck ached. Hector had bound her feet and hands, then tossed her over her buckskin gelding like a hundred-pound sack of oats. He used another piece of rope under the horse's belly to connect her feet and hands and keep her snug against the animal. She smelled like wet horse and mud. The wind, suddenly cold and harsh, numbed her face and fingers. Hannah's teeth chattered. The horse took another hard step. She groaned. At least the rain had stopped.

It was daylight now. They had ridden all night, though Hannah had been unconscious for much of the journey. The Apache kept the animals at a slow but steady pace, stopping only briefly to let the horses and mule catch their breath and graze a little. Hector had shown minimal concern for the animals, and none for Hannah—but that was to be expected. She wondered why he hadn't killed her.

Even more, she wondered what he had done with Cynthia. She refused to think the worst. Maybe she had escaped. Maybe that's why Hector had kidnapped her. He needed another hostage. Right now perhaps Cynthia was on a train heading back to Texas. Hannah would gladly make that trade, Cynthia for her. What was it that Pete or somebody had said? Apaches seldom killed their female captives. The gelding grazed a small pine, scratching Hannah's scalp and leaving strands of her blond hair wrapped around a branch. Well, this might be considered one form of torture. She quickly remembered the two men Hector had staked out on the West Texas plains and regretted her previous thought.

She felt the first flakes of wet snow sting her cheeks. *Great,* she thought, *now I will freeze to death.* Craning her neck, she could only make out Hector's straight back and his long hair blowing in the wind as he rode ahead, pulling the mule and Hannah's horse behind him. Her head felt like an anvil, and she dropped, banging her chin against the buckskin. She closed her eyes.

How she had fallen asleep, Hannah couldn't fathom a guess. She thought it must be approaching dusk, but maybe that was an illusion because of the trees and cloud cover. They were climbing higher into the mountains, on a steep trail now, and Hannah's horse had begun to labor. Snow still fell, but so far hadn't begun to stick. Pete would probably be on her trail now. That gave her some solace. She tried to flex her stiff fingers, to ward off frostbite. Her lips were cracking, and every time she took a deep breath, the frigid air burned her lungs. The gelding snorted.

Hannah suddenly became aware that all motion had stopped. She sensed movement beside her and turned, but Hector shoved her face against the buckskin. She glimpsed his knife and held her breath, but the blade sliced the rope on the underside of the animal. Hector sheathed the knife, straightened, and pushed Hannah off the horse.

She landed with crash and a curse, banging her head on a small rock. Hannah rolled over, her bound hands stretched out in front of her, and fought off tears. Hector laughed, the first sign of emotion he had shown. She shook her head, ground her teeth, and tried to think. Hector walked past her, knelt, took a firm grip on the rope binding her wrists with his right hand, and dragged Hannah through a mud puddle, over pine saplings, beside a pool of water at the base of a giant piece of granite, and into darkness.

The air felt cool and damp, not windy and freezing, and she realized she must be in a cave. "Stay," Hector said, and walked away.

Hannah lay on the cave floor. "Where do you think I'd go?" she said aloud, startled that she could speak. Something sounded to her right. Her head spun around toward the noise, bringing on a dizzy spell. She bit her lip. Bats? A bear? Suddenly she wished Hector would return. A timid voice called out:

"Mama Hannah?"

Hannah's heart pounded. "Cynthia!" she cried.

* * *

Pete woke up. He lay on top of satin sheets in his long underwear, clean-shaven but bruised, and, thankfully, with all of his long hair intact. He hadn't been scalped, at least. But where was he? Heaven? If that were the case, why did he hurt so much? He closed his eyes and shook his head, trying to think straight. He caught the aroma of lilac, a celestial scent he supposed, and . . . tobacco smoke? Somebody was smoking a cigarette in heaven?

Reality slowly took hold, and he realized he lay on top of a high bed.

"What the—"

"Hey, sugar, you're awake?"

He turned slowly. A redheaded woman smiled and flicked her smoke into a brass spittoon next to her chair. She was a big-boned gal with bloodshot green eyes and a couple of containers of rouge smeared on pasty cheeks. She wore a low-cut dress and, with a yawn, brought her bare feet onto the side of the bed. Pete was now certain heaven was not his present location. Maybe . . .

"Welcome to Calypso's Paradise, sugar," she said in a high-pitched, nasal Southern accent that, because she spoke so fast, was difficult to understand. "I'm Betty."

"Where am I?"

"Calypso's Paradise, sugar. Ain't you listenin'? The best saloon this side of St. Louis. I'm the owner."

She fired up another cigarette. "I suppose you ain't got a fair inklin' 'bout what happened to you."

Pete nodded.

"Well, you must have run afoul of Emilio Vasquez,

because we—we being me, George my bouncer, and
Stella, one of my girls—found you gettin' the tarna-
tion whopped out of you by that no-count, murderin'
swine and the Chumley brothers, Olaf and Grover.
They're about as mean as they come. Lucky for you
that George stands about six-foot-six and swings a
mean billy club, and I happened to be carryin' Bobby
Lee, my U.S. Arms double-barrel. That ol' scalphunter
and the Chumleys took off at a high lope, and we
brought you here. Vasquez picked the wrong place to
do his murderin'. I ain't havin' no potential customer
get hisself scalped before I get my two bucks. I run a
respectable establishment, the best in Hades. I reckon
you was on your way here when they jumped you.
Next time, sugar, come in the front door and don't
take to no alleys. Not in this town. How you feelin',
sugar? Hungry?"

He was starving. "I could eat. Some coffee maybe."

She cleared her throat and yelled. "George! The
gent's awake! Bring up some breakfast and a coffeepot, *muy pronto!*" Pete cringed at the noise.

Less than a minute later, the door slammed open.
George didn't tarry, Pete thought, but when he looked
up he saw three women move into the room and sit
on the bed. One, a petite Chinese wearing a jade necklace, brushed the bangs off his forehead and began
applying some salve on his battered face. Another, a
skinny brunette with a busted lower lip, patted his left
leg and cooed, "You po' thing." The third woman,
another brunette with dark eyes, rolled a cigarette and
stuck it in his lips.

"I don't smoke, ma'am," Pete said.

"Ma'am!" The skinny one cackled. "When's the last time you been ma'am'ed, Jeanne?"

Jeanne removed the cigarette for herself. "I got some snuff, precious," she offered.

"No thanks," he said.

"Mister," Betty said, "this is Jeanne, Stella, and Nien Chang."

Jeanne and Stella grinned. Nien Chang continued her treatment without speaking.

"What was that ol' Mexican killer and them big oafs doin' with you, anyway?" Stella asked.

"He was tryin' to kill him, stupid," Jeanne shot back. "What do you think?"

"I knower that, fool. But why?"

"They don't like me," Pete said, and forced a smile.

Jeanne, Stella, and Betty howled.

George tapped on the door frame. Betty hadn't lied. He was a giant black man, with a chest and arms bulging out of his muslin shirt, shaved head, and thick but neatly trimmed mustache and goatee. The three women moved out of the way as George entered the room. Belissari pushed himself up as the bouncer placed a tray holding a plate full of ham, eggs, and biscuits and a coffeepot and tin mug on Pete's lap. The man left without speaking.

Betty cleared her throat. "All right, gals, let this gent eat and rest."

Jeanne pouted. "That ain't rightly fair, Betty. Here's the first decent-lookin' fella we've had in months, even with his beat-up face. How come you get to hog him?"

"Because I own this place. Now git."

As soon as the door closed, Betty turned to Pete, who sipped the bitter coffee and tried a piece of burned ham. "I appreciate this, ma'am," Pete said, "but I wonder if I may impose on you again?"

"Gosh, you is a polite one. We don't get too many of your kind in Hades. Ask away, sugar."

"I left a gray mustang—"

"Already taken care of, sug. After we got you up to my room and let Nien Chang look at your wounds— she's a pretty good doc, and ain't near as expensive as some Santa Fe sawbones—I sent George to ask around 'bout you. Anyway, a couple of folks remembered you and we took your hoss to the livery. Leave a horse on these streets too long, and you'll find yourself afoot in a hurry. So don't you hurry. And don't worry none 'bout your horse, darlin'. You just fill your belly and get some rest. I'll come up to check on you later."

Pete found his clothes in Betty's armoire and quickly dressed. Vasquez or the Chumleys had taken his money and in all likelihood his Winchester. He pulled his hat down on his aching head as far as he dared and opened the door. Someone was snoring in the room across the hall. Belissari looked around and walked down the flimsy stairs. He found himself in a saloon. Across the room, George stood behind a bar, ravenously tearing the meat off a drumstick. The bouncer placed the bone on a plate and wiped his massive hands with a bar rag.

"Evenin'," he said in a low bass voice.

"George," Pete said and walked to the bar. "What time is it?"

"Half past five. Get enough to eat?"

"Yes. Thank you kindly."

The bouncer looked Pete over. "It ain't none of my affair, but are you goin' after them that ambushed you?"

Belissari shrugged. "Only if they come after me. Something else comes first."

"You be trailin' somebody?" Pete didn't answer. "You the law?"

Pete decided to be honest. "A ten-year-old girl was taken by a bronco Apache in Texas. I've been on their trail for months."

George tugged his goatee. "Apache. That would explain the scalphunter. If you're goin' into the mountains, you'll need a coat. Take mine. It's on the rack by the door."

"No . . ."

"Take it, I says. Else you'll freeze to death and never see that young'un of yours. This ain't Texas, mister. It gets mighty cold in the winter."

Pete thanked him. He saw the coat, tan canvas with a fleece collar that had seen considerable use and would swallow Belissari whole—even if it was four sizes too small for the bouncer—but at least it would keep Pete warm.

"You ain't plannin' on leavin' without sayin' good-bye to Miss Betty, is you?"

"Not at all," Pete lied. "Where is she?"

"I'll fetch her." Before leaving, George filled a shot glass from a bottle that said GLENLEVIT and pushed it toward Belissari. Pete took half a sip and as the liquor scalded his tongue and fried his throat, he knew the label on the bottle lied—this was no fancy whiskey. It didn't stop him from finishing the shot, however.

"Sugar!"

Belissari turned to see a grinning Betty run and give him a bear hug. "You must be feelin' better."

I was, Pete thought, and rubbed his sore ribs as Betty stepped aside.

"George tells me you're leavin'."

"Yes, ma'am," Pete said. "I'm afraid Vasquez robbed me, though. I want to pay you—"

"You'll do no such thing. You'll find your horse at Zachary's Livery. You tell him Miss Betty says to send her the bill. I treat my customers right. And the next time you're in Hades . . ." She gave him a kiss on the cheek, giggled, and left the parlor.

Pete Belissari felt his cheeks grow warm—and not because of the whiskey.

Chapter Nine

The man at Zachary's Livery didn't believe for one second that Miss Betty had said she'd foot the bill for boarding Poseidon, but he sent over a stableboy who confirmed the offer. Belissari rode Poseidon to the mercantile and went inside, where he told the clerk he wanted a gun and some ammunition but would have to barter. The pot-bellied clerk nodded. Bartering must have been common in a place like Hades. He led Belissari to a table that held an assortment of handguns, shotguns, and rifles.

Pete realized he didn't have much worth trading. "How about credit?" he asked.

The clerk smiled. "I don't give credit to my mama, Mac. That gray horse of yours might fetch you a Peacemaker, Henry, and two boxes of shells for each, though."

"That mustang is worth more than your entire store," Pete told him.

"You're the stranger that got taken by them Chumley boys, right?" Pete nodded. "I thought so. George was in here asking about you and that horse. Well, if you need a gun—and if the Chumleys are after you, you do need to be heeled—I'd suggest you go see our undertaker. You'll get a better deal from him than you will from me, unless you swap me that horse."

Pete thanked the man and asked where he could find the undertaker. "Stuart's Barber Shop," the clerk replied. "You could use a haircut, Mac, and you might be in need of an undertaker real soon. Stuart'll take care of you either way."

Stuart Sumner couldn't hide his disappointment when he found out he wouldn't get a chance to shear Pete's locks. He tugged on the ends of his well-waxed mustache and hooked the mound of tobacco from his cheek and into a spittoon before leading Pete, who carried his saddlebags over his shoulder, into the back room where several poorly constructed pine coffins leaned against the far wall, waiting for customers. One coffin sat balanced on two sawhorses. Inside lay a bearded man in buckskins with a knife wound in his chest.

Pete turned in disgust. "Not very fancy," he said.

"He got no complaints," Stuart said. "You can have the knife if you want. I couldn't get the blasted thing out."

"Like Excalibur," Pete said.

"Huh?"

"Never mind. Let's see the arsenal."

Stuart opened a Wells Fargo box and stepped back.

Belissari would have preferred a rifle, but apparently there were none for trade. He picked up a rusty old handgun. At first he thought it was a Navy .36, but he noticed the brass frame and knew it couldn't be a Colt. Probably one of the Confederate copies made during the war. He'd hate to fire the thing. It more than likely would blow his hand off. There was a Dragoon off of which some idiot had sawed the barrel, an assortment of derringers, a self-cocking Remington pocket model, and a long-barreled piece he had never seen before.

"Allen & Wheelock .38 lipfire," Stuart explained. "I took it off Lucky Dick after his luck played out."

"You know your guns," Pete said.

"You learn in this town."

"You know none of these is worth a spit."

"I know you ain't got much to trade for if Percy over at the mercantile sent you here."

Belissari thought that perhaps he should wait. Hannah still had his Remington. But what if he ran into Vasquez and the Chumleys on the trail? Finally, he set the saddlebags on the corpse's legs and opened one satchel. He didn't mean to be disrespectful of the dead, but it was the only thing resembling a table in the room. Pete pulled out a copy of *The Iliad* and handed it to Stuart.

"That's what I have to trade," Pete said.

Stuart shook his head. "A book? In Hades? Mister, that won't get you an empty shell casin'." The bartender-undertaker opened the book anyway. "By Jove, this thing ain't even written in English. It's full of squiggly circles and the like."

"It's written in Greek, and this is no ordinary book,"

Pete said. "It's *The Iliad* by Homer. Autographed. I really don't want to part with it, but I was told it's not wise to go around 'undressed' with the Chumley brothers and Emilio Vasquez gunning for you."

"That's the gospel truth, mister. I don't know that Vasquez gent, but the Chumleys are ugly and mean."

Pete stepped forward and turned the pages. He pointed out the fading inscription. Pete read:

" 'Sto epanidhín, Hrónia pollá. O patéras, Ho- mer.' "

"What's it mean?"

" 'I hope you enjoy reading this as much as I did writing it. Homer.' "

"Homer what?"

"Just Homer. Like Lucky Dick."

Stuart nodded. "I don't have much need for a book, even one with Homer's John Hancock on it. Besides, it's pretty old."

"It is. Homer lived about a thousand years before Christ was born."

That sold him. Stuart went to another box, went through it, and handed Pete a .44 Colt in a Mexican double-loop holster on a cartridge belt. "That's a Rich- ards conversion," he said. "Best gun you'll find in my collection. I'll throw in a box of shells and let you have a Bullard repeater, round barrel, in .50-115 cal- iber. That'll keep even Olaf and Grover Chumley down if you hit 'em. I'll give you some shells for that, too. Take it or leave it."

Pete took it, although he hated to part with the book. He looked at the inscription again, translating the words to himself this time: *"Until we see each other again. Happy birthday. Your father, Kostas."*

There wasn't much chance that someone in Hades could read Greek, but Pete left town at a gallop after swindling Stuart. He felt relieved to get out of the town, and wondered if Hannah would be worried. He stopped at the edge of the camp and knew something was wrong. Slowly, he pulled the Bullard rifle from the scabbard.

"It will snow this night," Hector said. "Hard. You should eat."

Hannah relented and chewed on a piece of dried meat that tasted like shoe leather. Maybe it was. She and Cynthia sat close to a small fire, while Hector stood near the entrance to the cave. He had brought in the horses and mule. Satisfied that his captives were eating, Hector turned his attention to the animals.

"Pete will be trailing us by now," Hannah whispered. "Don't worry. We'll be out of this in no time."

Cynthia smiled. She had been a regular trouper through this whole ordeal. She was sunburned and dirty, but not hurt. In fact, she said Hector had treated her fine once they got out of Texas. It had been hard going at first, and she had worried about Pete and Hannah when Hector had set up his ambush.

Hannah remembered the tortured Marfa men.

"Where were you when that happened?" she had asked earlier that evening.

"He"—Cynthia stuck out her jaw toward the brave, just as an Apache might—"tied me up and left me,

said I was too weak to watch what he would do. He-
he didn't chop . . . chop off anyone's head, did he?"

"No, child," Hannah said. "He injured a couple, but
no one got killed."

That might have been a stretch. For all Hannah
knew, Hector's two victims were six feet under by
now. And if they weren't dead, they probably wished
they were.

Now Hector walked toward the fire and squatted in
front of his captives. He tossed a couple of small
pieces of wood on the fire. "You white women get too
cold. You are not of The People, but you"—he indi-
cated Hannah—"you might be a worthy bride for a
true warrior. I will call you *Besdacada* because whoever takes you for his bride will say that word many,
many times."

Hannah decided to speak. *Be polite,* she told herself.
*Get on his good side. Make him trust you. Then per-
haps we can escape.*

"What does it mean?"

Hector smiled. "Nothing to put in your language. It
is, what you white eyes call, a cussword."

"You speak good English."

The Apache nodded. "They teach me at San Carlos.
Some of the soldiers teach me, too. And the scouts.
Al Sieber, he teach me some . . ." He looked at the top
of the cave. "I forget the name. '*Haben Sie zigarret-
ten*' and '*danke*.' "

Hannah didn't recognize the first phrase, but she
understood "*danke*." "It's German."

"Yes," Hector said. "German. So I go to the soldiers
that speak the language and say this. They give me a

smoke, and I say '*danke*.' It work pretty good. And, of course, I speak the language of the Mexicans. It is good for trade, though I do not like the Mexicans. Another bluecoat tried to teach me what he calls Irish, but I did not like the words."

"You're very smart," Hannah said. "I can only speak English." She could understand a little Spanish, and Pete had taught her a few words and phrases in Greek.

Hector frowned. "Not too smart. I trusted the blue-coats. I help them track my people. They put me in some railroad car like I see them load cows. I do not want to go to Flo-ri-da."

He stood and went to the packs. "I've never heard him talk so much," Cynthia said quietly.

"It's a good sign," Hannah said.

Hector returned with a canteen, which he offered to Hannah. She uncapped it and washed down the rough supper, then passed the container to Cynthia.

"She is *Le'i*," Hector said, looking at Cynthia. "It means 'one.' At first I called this one Weak White Girl, but she has become strong. She is only one per-son, and a girl at that, but she is enough."

Cynthia returned the canteen to Hector, who set it at his side. He stared at Hannah for a minute, then at Cynthia, not speaking. The silence, the man's haunting eyes—they combined to send a chill up Hannah's spine. She shivered, moved closer to the fire, and stared at the small flames.

"Yes," Hector finally spoke, "you both will make worthy gifts for the great Matitzal."

Hannah looked up. Matitzal? Where had she heard

that name before? Then she remembered. Pete had said Vasquez told him at the Mesilla jail that Hector would be going to join Matitzal, said that Matitzal had killed the scalphunter's family. But Dr. Leslie then informed Pete that Matitzal had been killed by Mexican troops during the War Between the States. Could Leslie have been mistaken? Could there be two Apaches named Matitzal?

"Hector?" Hannah waited, but the Apache simply stared at the back of the cave, seeing nothing, lost in thought. Hannah licked her lips and tried again. "Hector, where are you taking us?"

The Indian's eyes fell on Hannah. Maybe it was the poor lighting, but Hannah would later swear that the Apache's black eyes misted over.

"Home," he finally replied in a soft, faraway voice. "I am taking you home."

Chapter Ten

The tracks at the campsite, Pete knew, meant trouble. Three riders had churned up the muddy ground around the old cabin before taking off into the mountains. Belissari had a pretty good idea who those three men were: Vasquez and the Chumley brothers. But someone else had ridden off with Hannah's buckskin, the pack mule, and Hannah herself. This man wore moccasins. He had overpowered Hannah and kidnapped her. At least that's what Pete thought the signs said. He had to admit that tracking wasn't his best asset, but he could get by, especially if he was following a horse trail. Vasquez and his henchmen seemed to be following Hannah's captor.

And that, Pete surmised, meant it had to be Hector. Who else would Vasquez go after?

Belissari swore at himself for leaving Hannah alone in the wilderness but stopped himself. Hannah, he figured, wouldn't appreciate the thought. He imagined her argument: "I took pretty good care of myself long before I ever let you walk into my life, Petros Belissari, so don't think for one minute that just because I wear a dress I'm some weakling. It's not your fault I got caught by this Apache. It's mine. Besides, if you had been here, you'd be dead right this minute."

Well, Pete thought, *at least she's alive.*

At least, I think *she's alive.*

He sighed, said a silent prayer, and felt tears well in his eyes. *She's all right,* he told himself, but he couldn't stop worrying. He felt sick to his stomach.

There was no point in going after her now. It would soon be dark. He hobbled Poseidon nearby, gave the mustang a few oats, and made camp. Come first light, he'd follow the trail into the high country. He hoped to find them soon. Carrying only the food in his saddlebags and the beans and coffee he had picked up in Hades, Pete knew he wasn't outfitted for a long journey.

What else did he have? A weary mustang with only a few more oats for feed. A heavy coat way too big, and a dead man's pair of boots. Dead men's weapons, too, which he had procured by hoodwink if not actual thievery. Some jerky, coffee, and a little bit of grub. He sure could use that pack mule.

Hector slaughtered the mule two nights later and carved out steaks for supper while Hannah looked aghast. The animal had gone lame that day, and rather than leave the animal, Hector killed it. He left the pack saddle near the dead animal's body and rifled through it, emptying a flour sack and filling it with the five remaining cans of peaches. The bacon and salt pork he left to rot. Nor did the clothes, not even the ammunition, interest him. He only wanted peaches. Hannah couldn't quite grasp that.

They made camp a few miles from the slaughtered beast, and Hector roasted the meat, skewered with sticks, over a fire. The Apache handed rare pieces of mule to his captives. Cynthia took her supper without complaint. She blew on it a few times before tearing off a piece. Juice dripped down her chin.

Hannah stared in disbelief. She turned to the stick she held—she didn't even remember taking it from Hector—and looked up at the Apache.

"Eat," he ordered. "Is good."

Hannah sniffed the food. She studied Cynthia for a second and asked, "You like this?"

The girl swallowed. "I'm hungry. I've eaten a lot of stuff I never thought I'd touch since I've been with Hector, Mama Hannah. You better eat."

Hannah took a tentative bite. The sizzling meat burned the roof of her mouth, and she quickly swallowed. It really wasn't bad, she finally decided, if you could overlook the fact that it was mule meat, and Hannah was famished.

For the first time in her life, Hannah Scott went to sleep with a belly full of mule. She woke up the next morning covered with snow.

Belissari knew he was on the right trail. Only by accident had he seen strands of Hannah's blond hair on a pine branch, but that was enough. Maybe she had torn it out herself to leave as a trail marker. Horse droppings he found in a cave where they must have camped, and the following day he found small footprints besides the ones he knew Hannah must have left. Cynthia! It had to be her.

But there were other signs, too, and those were discomforting. Vasquez and the Chumleys were also on Hector's trail, and they had at least a day's head start on Belissari.

Wolves had made good work of the dead mule, scattering bones among the rocks. Pete swung off Poseidon and looked at the contents emptied from the pack saddle. The wolves had consumed the bacon. "Gluttons," Pete said aloud. "Wasn't an entire mule enough to satisfy you?" He found a can of tomatoes nearby, opened it with a knife, and ate ravenously, like a wolf himself. Somehow, Hector (and Vasquez and the Chumleys, too, if they had bothered to stop) had overlooked a few things, though. And so had the wolves.

The ammunition wouldn't fit his new weapons, so he left the boxes behind, but he stuffed jerky, hardtack, salt pork, and as much canned goods as his saddlebags would hold. He also found a bag of oats, which he strapped behind the cantle of his saddle.

"I hate to weigh you down, boy," he whispered to the mustang. "But I don't think you'll mind the oats."

"Sit," Hector spoke harshly. "With your backs to each other."

Hannah and Cynthia did as they were told. The Apache squatted beside them and tied their hands with a long strip of rawhide. Hannah bit her lip as the leather bit into her wrists. Hector hadn't tied her up since the first night in the cave. Hannah figured it wasn't because he trusted Hannah and Cynthia; he just was confident they couldn't get past him. The fact was Hannah had never seen the Apache sleep. She knew he had to, but he never seemed to doze when his captives were awake. So why were they being bound? Why do it now, in the morning when they should be breaking camp?

Hector must have read her mind. "We are being trailed," he said. "The time is right to kill."

Pete! Hannah almost gasped. "Hector," she pleaded, "you can't do this. You can't—"

His right hand pressed hard against her lips. "Silence," he said, "or I will gag the both of you." He smiled wickedly then. "Besides, you better hope I do the killing. If I die, then you might not be found and will feed the wolves, bears, and ravens."

He tied Cynthia's and Hannah's feet with rope before picking up the bow and arrows he had fashioned the previous night. Hannah remembered him making the weapons. "Why do you need those?" Cynthia had asked. "They kill quietly," Hector had answered. Now the Apache walked out of view, carrying the silent killers, leaving the horses in camp. As soon as he had disappeared, Hannah struggled against the bonds, but the leather only seemed to tighten. She gave up after a few long minutes, exhausted from the thin air and cold.

It began to snow, softly at first, then wet flakes driven by a hard wind. Hannah tried again to free herself, but it was no use. "I'm freezing, Mama Hannah," the girl cried. Hannah tried to soothe Cynthia. "It'll be all right," she said.

"Tell me a story," Cynthia said. "Please."

"What would you like to hear?"

"How 'bout how you and Pete first met?"

Hannah smiled. "You know that one. You were there."

"Tell me anyway."

"We were doing chores," Hannah began. "It was a Friday in May, and all of a sudden I looked up toward Wild Rose Pass and saw this man riding like crazy, pulling—"

"Christopher saw him first."

"That's right, he did."

"He was being chased by Indians. He thought they were after him, but they weren't. They were good Indians. I wish Hector was a good Indian."

"So do I."

Pete heard the scream. Instinctively, he pulled the Bullard from the scabbard and jacked in a shell. *You're getting careless,* he told himself. *You should have had a shell in the chamber and the rifle across your lap. Mistakes like this get people killed.* He swung out of the saddle, wrapped the reins around a pine branch, and scrambled up some rocks. He unbuttoned his heavy coat to give himself more freedom. Pete leaned against a tree and peered into the small meadow below. It was snowing, but not hard, so he could see. A rider galloped like a madman, looking behind him while whipping his horse mercilessly with long reins.

Emilio Vasquez. Pete could make out the grizzled vaquero. The scalphunter was scared to death. But where were the Chumley brothers? Vasquez disappeared. He wouldn't get far at that pace; the horse would soon play out. Pete stared below, but no one followed. Belissari never thought he would see the old Mexican run like that. What could have scared him so? A grizzly? Perhaps. Hector? Or was Vasquez setting a trap, leaving the Chumleys hidden somewhere to ambush Pete?

Pete slid down the rocks, fetched the hobbles from his saddlebag, and left Poseidon in the small canyon, safe from the wind and snow, with a little bit of forage. He moved ahead slowly, cautiously, from pine to pine. His lips felt numb, and the deerskin gloves didn't offer much protection from the cold. He would pick his way down into the meadow and see if he could find the cause of Vasquez's terror.

The forest turned thick and confining like a jail cell. Pete tried to control his breathing, slowly, in and out through his nose. Silence disturbed him. The only sound came from towering pines rustling in the wind and his boots sinking into ankle-deep snow. He longed for a drink of water, but his canteen remained on the saddle.

What was that? He jerked the rifle up, pressed the stock against his shoulder, sighted over the barrel, tracing a slow path with the repeater from tree to tree, half expecting to see one of the Chumleys, or Hector, aiming back at him. He saw nothing, though, and slowly lowered the barrel. A limb to his right creaked and dumped a hatful of snow onto the ground.

Maybe that was all it was. He stepped from the tree, put his right boot on top of a fallen tree, testing his footing, and pulled his left leg behind him. A stone rattled to his left. He swung the barrel again, caught movement to his right. A trick! And old trick at that. Pete tried to correct his mistake, knew he was too late, and felt his feet slip on the bark. A split second later his legs had sailed out from under him, the Bullard flew from his gloved, cold hands, and Belissari landed with a splat in a sitting position.

His teeth snapped together, hurting his jaw, and he winced as pain shot up his spine from his tailbone to his neck. The rifle landed just a few feet from him, disappearing in the snow.

Hector!

The Apache appeared from nowhere, pulling back a taut bowstring. Pete swore, reached for the rifle . . . The next thing he knew, he was leaning against the fallen tree. One second he had been trying to pick up the Bullard, the next his right hand gripped the end of an arrow shaft, his hands crushing the feathers. Pete looked down and saw the arrow just below his ribs. Blood warmed his shirt, staining the deerskin gloves. Hector walked toward him, notching another arrow into his bow.

Pete reached again for the rifle but had barely moved before he cried out in pain. He could hardly move. Belissari took a sharp breath, reached for the revolver, and froze. Hector stood over him, an arrow aimed right for his heart.

Belissari met the Apache's stare. He didn't blink, didn't even breathe. He expected the arrow to fly any second, but slowly Hector lowered the bow and returned the arrow into a makeshift quiver. The Indian snatched the Colt from the holster and tossed it away. He picked up the rifle, studied it for a second, then also pitched it far from the horseman's reach.

"I should kill you," Hector said. "But I have a better idea." Using Pete's bandanna and a piece of rope, Hector tied Pete's hands to the trees on both sides of him. The Apache nodded, satisfied.

Tying his hands wasn't necessary, Pete thought. He couldn't move anyway. Belissari knew he was a dead man.

"My horse," Pete said dryly. "Hobbled in the canyon not far from here. Take him."

"I don't want your horse, Dark Eyes," Hector said. "The wolves may eat him, after they consume you."

Chapter Eleven

Hector led the horses to the picket line: a short-coupled frost appaloosa; a powerful Tennessee Walker, roan mare with white markings; and a gray mustang Hannah would recognize anywhere. Her stomach turned, her lips quivered, and blood rushed to her head. "Mama Ha—" Cynthia began, but Hannah silenced her with a harsh command. The girl began to sob.

Finished with the horses, the Apache walked into camp, leaned his bow and quiver against a tree, withdrew his knife, and freed the ten-year-old first. "Apaches do not cry," he spoke angrily, and shoved the girl into the snow. He stared at the trembling orphan for a few seconds, then glared at Hannah.

She kept her composure. She had to. "What happened?" she asked tightly. It was difficult. She flexed her fingers, ground her teeth, and tried not to look at Poseidon.

Hector laughed. "Three White Eyes will feed the worms come spring," he said. "One got away, but he will ride his horse into the ground and freeze to death in this country." Hannah suddenly held out hope. Perhaps Pete had found a posse in Hades. Maybe he had gotten away on someone else's horse.

Gesturing to Poseidon, Hector continued, "The fool who owned this horse I left for the wolves. He asked me to take his horse." Hector nodded, maybe out of respect for Pete. "At first I thought I had no need for another horse, but I sought him to see for myself. He is a good horse. I might keep him for myself."

"What . . ." Hannah had to take a deep breath. "What about . . . the owner?"

"I left him for the wolves to finish. By now he is dead."

He reached down and cut Hannah free, hovering over her for a second, trying to read the thoughts in her eyes.

Hannah bit her lip and brought both hands up quickly, slamming them palm first into the brave's throat. Hector straightened, shocked, fighting for air. The knife fell into the mushy snow. Hannah ignored it. She jumped up, let out a savage curse, and kicked hard, catching the retreating Apache in his right knee. He went down, rolled up, came up quickly, black eyes full of hatred now.

But he still couldn't breathe.

Her joints and muscles had stiffened from the cold and lack of movement. She fought for breath herself, turned, and reached for the knife. It was hard to pick up. Her fingers didn't want to work. Hannah cried out in desperation, finally got a grip on the bone handle, and swung around. Hector punched her. The knife sailed one way, Hannah the other. She landed near a tree and tried to get up, but the Apache knocked her down. His fingers clasped her throat. She fought for air, helpless. The black eyes locked on her, concentrating, his face masked in fury. Hannah's right arm stretched out and her fingers felt through the snow, touching something. Canvas. A bag. She held out hope. Hector's quiver. She moved upward, fingered a shaft and feathers. Yes. Quickly she gripped the shaft, pulled the arrow out—

Hector realized what she was doing. He loosened his stranglehold, turned too late, and let out a surprisingly feminine yelp as the stone arrowhead ripped into his calf. He rolled off, gripping his bloody leg.

Hannah came to her knees. Her chest heaved as the thin air filled and burned her lungs. It was hard to see. Everything seemed blurry at first, but she soon regained focus. She glanced at the writhing Apache, saw him yank the arrow from his leg, try to stand, slip, mumble something in a guttural voice.

A gun. That's what she needed. Hannah turned toward the animals and saw the stock of a rifle in the saddle scabbard on the Tennessee Walker. She bolted for the horse and heard footsteps and grunts behind her.

The roan shied away from her, panic in her eyes. Hannah touched the stock but before she could unsheathe the rifle, a vise clenched her left shoulder and flung her backward. She slid in the snow. Pain shot through down her arm and up her neck. Hector stumbled toward her. The horses whinnied and stomped the snow nervously.

Hannah sat up and reached into the snow with both hands. Good, her shoulder wasn't broken. She hoped to find a rock, but there was only snow and frozen ground. Hector kicked at her with his left foot, but she dodged the blow. He, too, gasped for air. He swore in English, then said something she couldn't understand and reached for her throat once more.

A rock smashed his nose, spraying blood. Hector reached out instinctively toward his face, and turned to his left.

"Leave her alone!" Cynthia shouted. "You killed Pete!"

He dodged another rock, then charged the girl.

"No!" Hannah cried out weakly. She rolled over, pulled herself to her feet, and tumbled after him.

Hector had just thrown Cynthia to the ground when Hannah's injured shoulder connected with the small of his back. He grunted. Both fell hard. Hannah rolled over and tried to get up, but couldn't.

She closed her eyes, summoning a final surge of energy. . . .

The Apache fell on top of her again. This time he had recovered his knife. The cold blade pressed against her throat. Hector glanced once at Cynthia, but the girl lay unmoving on the ground, unconscious.

He panted, wiped his face with his left hand, and glared. The blade went deeper. Hannah was glad Cynthia was knocked out. She wouldn't see her die.

Suddenly, Hector laughed and withdrew the knife.

"Besdacada," he said hoarsely. "I named you well."

* * *

Hector treated his wounds and tied Hannah and Cynthia up again. He didn't feed them that night nor the next morning when they broke camp. He put Cynthia on the appaloosa and Hannah on Poseidon, binding their hands tightly to the saddle horns. He used a rope to string the animals together, mounted his horse, and pulled them along.

This went on for two more days, although he let his captives eat again the following afternoon. On the third morning, Hannah smelled wood smoke and saw the Apache cautiously pull out his rifle. The scent became stronger as they continued. Ten minutes later, a sharp voice barked from the trees. Hector reined to a halt. He did not raise the rifle.

Hannah had prayed that they were nearing a camp of white hunters, maybe even soldiers, but the voice had been in a language she couldn't understand.

A smiling Apache appeared, loosely holding an old breech-loading rifle. He wore a strange-looking cap with rawhide ears and a frayed Army greatcoat over his buckskins. A silk neckerchief, decorated with silver conchos, hung around his neck. Strands of silver gave his shoulder-length black hair a salt-and-pepper look.

He spoke to Hector, who smiled and sheathed the rifle. Hector responded with a few grating words. Ear Hat nodded and walked down the line of horses, patting the Walker's neck in admiration, before stopping in front of Cynthia. He said something to Hector, who responded curtly, and Ear Hat focused on Hannah. His eyes fell to her bound hands. Grinning widely, he turned back toward Hector and said:

"Which one uglied your face?"

The words, spoken in English, surprised Hannah.

Hector spoke harshly, in Chiricahua, Hannah guessed, and kicked his horse forward. The sentry, snickering, followed on foot.

Hannah had never seen an Apache *ranchería*. A fire pit rested in the center of camp, and a few old women sat around the flames, staring at Hector and his captives. The women said nothing.

Several wickiups made of cottonwood poles, yucca, and beargrass circled the compound. Two children played in the snow in front of a brush arbor, and a few other men and women stepped from inside the huts and looked at the parade in silence. Hector halted in front of a wickiup on the far side of camp. He kept quiet. Hannah licked her lips. Finally, the beargrass covering flew open, and a humpbacked man exited and stood in front of Hector.

The man wore a straw hat, about two sizes too small, on top of his head, and thick white hair reached to the collar of a black woollen vest that covered a buckskin shirt. His pants were loose white cotton, the bottoms covered with his leggings and moccasins, and he held a long lance, taller than Hannah herself, painted black near the top, decorated with strips of red silk and feathers where the long silver blade was attached.

His face was flat, wrinkled and rather plump, with dark eyes set close to a pudgy nose, and narrow, unsmiling lips. He could have been anywhere between sixty and six hundred years old.

Hector dismounted and began speaking in rapid Chiricahua, gesturing toward the horses. The old man didn't move, didn't even blink, as Hector had Ear Hat lead the Walker past the ancient Apache first, then parade Cynthia and Hannah by. But the chief—at least, Hannah assumed he was the chief—paid no attention to horses or captives. His eyes locked on Hector.

The brave sighed, looked around uncertainly, spoke again, and fell silent.

"Do'a," the ancient one said.

Hector continued, but the only words Hannah understood were *Besdacada* and *Le'i*. When Hector had finished, Ancient One handed the lance to Ear Hat and examined the Tennessee Walker, checking the mare's teeth like an old horse-trader, then moving on to Cynthia. He spoke a deep command. Hector cut the rawhide strip that held the child to the saddle and helped her dismount. The girl wouldn't even look up at Ancient One; she simply stared at her feet, until the old chief's right hand pushed her jaw up.

"Le'i," Hector said, and began another rapid, deep sales pitch to the Apache leader.

Ancient One nodded slightly and moved toward Hannah. Hector cut her loose, and she slid from the saddle, rubbing her wrists, and looked at the old man. Hector fired off a few other sentences. This time, Ancient One smiled. He pointed toward Hector's broken, swollen nose, and asked something.

Hector shuffled his feet, stuttered, and looked at the

snow-covered ground. He finally answered quickly but softly, pointing at Cynthia.

Led by Ancient One, the entire village broke out laughing.

The chief raised his hand, and the laughter stopped. Hector took a deep breath before raising his head. Ancient One spoke again, first to Hector, then to one of the boys. The youth scrambled forward and led the Walker away. Next the chief raised his arms and began a long speech. When he was finished, a cheer went up and the old women surrounding the fire pit began to sing. Several braves led Poseidon and the other horses to the horse herd. Hector and the old man walked to the fire pit. Someone began to beat a drum. Another child started dancing, and the adults either followed Hector and Ancient One or returned to their wickiups.

Hannah looked at Cynthia. Everyone seemed to have forgotten about the white captives in the Apache *ranchería*. Everyone, that is, except Ear Hat. The man grunted.

"Mexicans call me Sabana," he said. "You, too, call me Sabana. It easy. Name The People give me you no can say."

"What's going on?" Hannah asked.

"Feast tonight. *Muy grande* celebration. Drink *tiz-win*. Dance. He Who Chops Off The Heads Of His Enemies come home."

"What about us?"

Sabana motioned to Ancient One's wickiup. "Go inside. Rest. You now belong to Matitzal, great leader of the Bedonkohe."

Hannah whispered the name. So it was true. Matitzal. Maybe he hadn't been killed in Mexico during the war.

"*Sí*, Matitzal. His only son come home today. Go. Eat. Sleep."

Hannah took Cynthia by the hand and led her inside Matitzal's hut. So Hector was the chief's son. She wondered what the old man would do to her when she killed the swine for murdering Pete.

Chapter Twelve

Supper had been horse meat—Hannah hoped the Apaches hadn't butchered Poseidon—yucca fruit, berries, and the cans of peaches, which Matitzal consumed greedily, draining the juice. The men dipped gourds into a brass kettle and chugged down this *tizwin.* "Gray water," Sabana explained as he offered Hannah the beverage. The three stood near Matitzal's wickiup, away from the loud singing and wild dancing around the fire pit. *The prodigal son comes home,* Hannah thought, *and what a celebration.* She tried not to think about Pete. Instead she thought about somehow sneaking Cynthia out and finding the horse herd.

Tizwin felt sticky and tasted like fermented corn, some sort of sweet beer. It must have been intoxicating because some of the men were weaving, mumbling, and falling to the ground. Or perhaps they were just dizzy from dancing in circles.

"It feeds body," Sabana said, nodding at the drink.

"Can make sick, though. Let children drink because we have little food. That why tonight we eat the old mare of Antelope Who Kills With His Eyes."

Good, Hannah thought. They weren't supping on Poseidon.

Sabana nodded. "We will stay here until spring. It safe. Whites no look for us here. Then continue journey."

"Where are you going?" Hannah asked.

"Matitzal will explain."

She considered this. If they were eating horse meat now in November, what would they be forced to consume in the coming months? Hannah put the question to Sabana.

"There are wood rats," he said, "and rabbits, some elk. We can go into the White Man's country and steal some of his cows. We have mescal and squash, berries and dried meat. Plenty of *tizwin* and juice from beans of mesquite. Other meat can be found in mountains."

"Bears and coyotes?" Cynthia asked in disgust.

"Never," he answered. "They carry evil spirits. You will learn, *Le'i*, of our taboos. Turkeys eat worms, so no eat turkeys. Fish are slimy like the snake, so no eat fish."

"Good," Cynthia said. "I don't like fish, neither, except for the fried tails Mama Hannah makes after Paco and Chris catch some in the creek. They're crunchy and salty."

A few hours later, the celebration began to die down, and old Matitzal slowly approached the wickiup. He motioned Hannah, Cynthia, and Sabana inside. They sat cross-legged in a circle, and the two men shared a pipe for several minutes. By the time the chief began to speak, Cynthia had fallen asleep. Matitzal spoke in Apache, complementing his short, throaty sentences with hand gestures. But even then, Hannah couldn't figure out anything he was saying. When Matitzal had finished, he stared at Hannah as Sabana explained.

"In beginning," Sabana said, "world is without death because of Raven. Raven say if he throw stick in water and stick no sink, then there no be death. If stick sinks, world has death. Stick floats, and Raven glad. But then come Coyote. Coyote takes stone and says if he throw stone in water and stone no sink, there no be death. But if stone sinks, death will be. Coyote throws stone in water. Stone sinks. This is why there is death in world."

Silence fell for a few seconds. Hannah could see the resemblance to Hector in Matitzal's dark eyes. The old man grunted and spoke again. When he was finished, Sabana again translated:

"So world of The People has death. And more death come at hands of Mexicans and soldiers in blue, other White Eyes. Many names we never say again. We no speak names of those gone to live with fathers and mothers. We war against ourselves. Own son, who you call Hector, is a wolf for bluecoats. It is bad day for The People. We are *Indeh*. We are The Dead."

Another pause. Then a longer speech from the chief. Sabana cleared his throat and spoke:

"We fought hard, but White Eyes and Mexicans are like sand. Too many. War hard on children. We grow old. Tired. And then I hear of the great leader of Lakota, *Tatanka-Iyotanka* he is known among his people. Sitting Bull, White Eyes call him. He has made peace in place called Grandmother's Country. Soldiers of this Grandmother's Country no kill his children. No burn his wickiups. They honorable, not like bluecoats and Mexicans.

"This where I take my people to live, where I will die. I rather die in the country of my father's father, but this cannot be. Perhaps *Tatanka-Iyotanka* will let us live among his people. I no know. But Lakota not enemy, so I feel good. It long journey north to Grandmother's Country. I send word to son, but too late. He put on iron horse with others, gone to this Flo-ri-da. With weary heart, I move from Mexico to join Lakota.

"But winter will be hard. Sunflowers tell me that. We rest here, close to old hunting grounds. When snow melt, we go on. North. You, *Besdacada*, and *Le'i,* the little one, come with us. You help us find *Tatanka-Iyotanka* and Grandmother's Country. You speak language of White Eyes. This help. Maybe you speak language of Lakota. I not know. But you help. For this, I pay you with horses and robes, with my heart. I no treat you or *Le'i* poorly. That is all. I have spoken."

Matitzal nodded. Sabana left the wickiup. Hannah and the ancient Apache stared at each other briefly, not speaking. Finally, the chief pointed to woollen blankets behind her. A bed. She covered Cynthia and pulled another blanket, stamped U.S. ARMY, over herself. The Apache grunted and went to sleep instantly, snoring like an old dog.

Sitting Bull? Grandmother's Country? Did Matitzal

really think he could lead his people from Mexico all the way to Canada? And didn't he know that the Sioux warrior had left Canada years ago, had surrendered to the Army and was now living on a reservation in Dakota Territory?

Well, she thought, she had a better chance to escape if they were pushing north, if they were wintering here in the mountains. If she could earn the old man's trust, maybe she could somehow get Cynthia out of here before winter set in. And she hadn't forgotten about Hector. She still planned to avenge Pete's death.

Hannah sat upright in a start. As her vision cleared, she realized she was no longer in Matitzal's wickiup. As far as she could see stretched snow-covered plains. She wore her ragged dress, out in the open. The wind blew, yet she didn't feel cold. The sky was black, the snow white, with no other colors. "Cynthia!" she called out.

But she was alone.

She heard Pete's voice. Hannah's heart skipped, and she turned. Beside her sat Coyote, wagging tail sweeping the snow, yellow eyes and long snout giving him a mischievous countenance. He was plump, probably from raiding Hannah's chicken coop again.

"You should have married him," Coyote said, sounding just like Pete. "Now you'll never get the chance. He is dead, you know."

"I know," Hannah said, and she started to cry. Her tears turned to ice and sank below the snow.

"Pity," said Coyote, and he laughed.

"Now you're all alone." He licked his lips. "Maybe

I should eat you myself. Before you get too skinny from living with *Indeh* all winter." He growled, sounding like a bear, and sprang at her.

Hannah ducked. She expected to feel his claws slash her, feel the fangs tear into her neck. She straightened. Coyote loped past her. A giant rabbit stood in the distance. *No wonder he has forgotten about me*, Hannah thought. *Rabbit is a much better meal. Only . . .*

Rabbit didn't move. He looked strange. Coyote didn't notice and his teeth sank into a leg.

"Owww!" Coyote yelped, sounding like Pete the time he had been kicked by that blood-red stallion, sounding like a baby. Hannah smiled at the memory. Pete could act like a ten-year-old at times.

Tears flowed again.

Coyote cursed. "Rabbit is made of rock!" he yelled.

Hannah looked for Coyote, but he had vanished. So had Rabbit.

Her tears stopped. The snow melted and faded away. Hannah sat on a bench outside the Pantheon. She didn't know how she realized this was the Pantheon. She had never been to Greece, only as far north as Kansas, as far west as Arizona, and as far east as Missouri.

"Why do you cry, my child?"

The soft voice soothed her. She looked up into the clear gray eyes of the most beautiful woman Hannah had ever seen. She wore armor and a helmet like those of Roman soldiers Hannah had seen in storybooks. Her shield was polished, mesmerizing, yet her staff resembled the Apache lance Matitzal had carried. A rooster rested on the shield. A snake crawled up the shaft.

An owl hooted.

Hannah trembled.

"Fear not," the woman said. "I am Athena, goddess of wisdom and the arts, born fully grown from the head of my father, Zeus."

Hannah swallowed. *"Hriázome voíthia,"* Hannah said. *Strange*, she thought. *I'm speaking Greek.*

"Why do you need help?" the goddess asked.

Hannah sobbed again. "Hector killed my Petros," she said. "Now I'm alone with Cynthia in an Apache camp. They want me to lead them to Canada. I . . . I just want to go home. And, forgive me, I want to kill Hector."

Athena's touch stopped Hannah's tears. She felt warm. "Come here, dear child, and sit beside me."

They were in the dining room at the Lempert Hotel back in Fort Davis. Hannah's ragged dress had been replaced with a brocaded silk suit, and Athena wore a spotless white robe instead of armor.

"Why do you think Petros is dead?" the goddess asked.

"Coyote told me. Hector told me."

"Coyote is a trickster, child. Hector lies, also. You have nothing to fear, Hannah Scott."

"But . . ."

"Petros, son of Kostas and Calliope Belissari, lives. I have sent a *gahe* to him. He is weak, but he does not die. You will see him again, but only if you prove yourself worthy to Zeus. Winter will be long and hard. Cynthia and the Apaches will need you. You cannot lead them to Canada. You know that is a mistake. You know many, if not all, will die on such a journey. Their place is at Mount Ida. This is where they will find peace. You must lead them there."

"But I've never heard of Mount Ida."

"And you won't. But you will recognize it by another name."

Hannah tried to understand. They had left the Lempert and now stood alone on a beach as waves crashed onto the white sands and gulls sang songs.

Athena held up a long, delicate finger. Her voice turned strong.

"Hear my warning, child. You must not harm Hector. He is a spearman and a fighter, and we marvel at him. Hector will die at the hands of Achilles, but that you will not see. Hector is not your enemy. That is the beast cyclops. Remember this. Now go, Hannah Scott. Know that Petros Belissari lives, and will live as long as you please the gods."

Hannah's eyes opened. It was morning, and bitterly cold. She lay in the wickiup, relaxed, remembering. It had been only a dream, but somehow she knew Pete lived. She threw off the covers and looked around. Matitzal was gone. She smelled wood smoke and food, heard wood being chopped and the melodious language of the Apaches. Hannah shook Cynthia awake, eager to tell her about the dream, about her strange yet wonderful feelings.

The ten-year-old rubbed her eyes.

"Guess what?" Hannah said.

Cynthia yawned. Hannah didn't wait for a reply.

"Pete's alive. I can't explain, honey. I just feel it."

"I know, Mama Hannah," Cynthia said sleepily. "Athena just told me."

Chapter Thirteen

By the second day, Pete figured he wasn't bleeding to death from the arrow wound. Maybe the freezing temperatures had caused that. He didn't know; he wasn't a doctor. And he wasn't sure it was for the best. If he had died, he would be out of pain. Now his death became a long affair. The bleeding had stopped—at least, he thought it had stopped—but now he faced frostbite . . . infection . . .

And the wolves.

He had heard their mournful cries each night, but so far they hadn't discovered him. Pete had managed to free both of his hands the morning after Hector had left him, but he couldn't pull the arrow out. He remained immobile bait for wolves, bears, or ravens. By now, Belissari had weakened considerably. Even if he could remove the arrow, he would never be able to crawl to Poseidon—if the mustang still lived—mount up, and ride to get help. For days, he had melted snow in his hand and drank. His lips were cracked. His fingers were numb. He no longer could move his legs.

Belissari wasn't used to failure. And he certainly hadn't considered his mortality often. He thought about the copy of *The Iliad* he had given the barber-undertaker back in Hades. A birthday present. He thought about his mother and her standard birthday greeting to him: *Na ta katostísis. May you live to be a hundred.* Well, he would come up about seventy years short. He thought about Hannah. Why hadn't he married her? *"Agape mou,"* he whispered aloud, the first words he had spoken since yesterday. *My love.* He figured those would be his final words on Earth.

Petros Belissari would die alone in these mountains. There would be no *kóllyva*, the memorial dish, symbolizing the eternal circle, of boiled wheat, sugar, and spices. No *makaría*, the meal after the funeral to bless the dead. No communion or the three Holies. No forty-day mourning. Well, he wasn't sure he deserved forty days of mourning. No grave either.

He hoped he faced the east. Pete couldn't tell, but among his people bodies were to be buried on consecrated soil facing east. Maybe he had consecrated this land with his blood.

Hannah and Cynthia would be with Hector. Belissari had failed. He didn't know what the Apache would do with his captives. Kill them? Turn them into slaves? Soon, it wouldn't be Pete's concern. *I wonder if they are as cold as I am?* he thought. It had snowed often since Hector had left him here. Was he cold because he was dying? Or was it because of the wind and snow?

Something rattled in the bushes. Pete looked up and tried to swallow but couldn't.

Wolves.

If he wasn't dying, he would soon be dead.

He mouthed a silent prayer, prepared to face his judgment, closed his eyes, and waited for the animals. Snow crunched. Seconds passed. A shadow crossed over him. Hot breath warmed his face. A horse snorted.

Horse—Poseidon? Pete opened his eyes. His gray mustang didn't look down at him. It was the face of a man, with a massive gray beard, stained at the corners of the mouth from tobacco juice, that stretched to his wide belt. Gray eyes. Bronze cheeks, nose, and forehead. Dingy leather hat. Buckskins and an unbuttoned buffalo coat. Behind him stood a broad-backed chestnut Morgan carrying an elk carcass behind a Denver rig.

Startled to see Pete was still alive, the man jumped back, recovered, glanced at the arrow, then looked back at Belissari.

"By Jehoshaphat!" he bellowed. "Does that hurt?"

If Pete could have reached up, he would have strangled the idiot right then and there.

She had waited too long. Hannah stepped outside the wickiup to a stark, white world. Wet snow continued to fall, topping Sabana's medicine hat so that he resembled a circus clown rather than a bronco Apache warrior. Sabana, Matitzal, Hector, and two other men stood in a circle beside a wood pile, their faces hidden by frosty vapors as they spoke animatedly. Hannah

sighed heavily. Escape for Cynthia was impossible.
She couldn't send the child out in this weather, which
had no intention of letting up any time soon.

They were stuck here . . . for the rest of winter.

Sabana saw her first. He must have said something,
because a second later all eyes locked on Hannah. She
recognized Matitzal's unmistakable voice and watched
uneasily as Sabana approached her.

"What's the matter?" Cynthia asked.

"I don't know. Go back inside the wickiup. Wait
for me."

"Hoddentin's oldest bride very sick," Sabana said.
"I try all my powers, but worms still eat her lungs.
Matitzal says perhaps you have great power. You re-
mind him of White Painted Woman, very holy, only
her child, Child of the Water, is boy and your child,
Le'i, is girl. Still, you look at Nah-dos-te, no?"

Hannah nodded, and she followed Sabana across the
camp, aware of the men staring at her. Snow swallowed her feet past the ankles, and the wind bit
through her clothes. She shivered as they continued on
past the horse herd—Poseidon snorted at her—and to
a lone wickiup. Sabana held opened the bear-grass
covering and followed her inside.

The old woman—what was the name Sabana called
her? Nah-dos-te?—had wasted away to skin and
bones. She lay shaking beneath several robes, hollow
eyes, pale skin, blood on her lips. Nah-dos-te coughed
harshly. Hannah gasped and covered her own nose and
mouth with her left arm.

Consumption!

The woman looked up and choked out something

in the hard tongue of the Apache. Hannah didn't understand the words but she could read Nah-dos-te's eyes, pleading for help, praying for a quick end to the pain. She lay dying, and there was little Hannah could do. Her instincts were to run out of the wickiup as fast as she could, to get away from the contagious killer and breathe fresh, clean air in the frigid outside. But Hannah couldn't do it. She had never been able to shun the helpless.

She knelt by the frail woman, taking the calloused, weathered left hand in her own—although Hannah still kept her nose and mouth covered.

"It'll be all right," she whispered. "It'll be all better soon."

Consumption meant death. Hannah knew this. The old woman realized she was dying, too. Hannah tried to think. A lot of consumptives came to West Texas because of the dry climate, and she had heard some of the remedies they used to ease the deterioration of the lungs. But what were they? Ginger root. Yes, that was one, but they would be hard-pressed to find that here. She snapped her fingers. Oak bark, mixed with honey and boiled into a tea. It wouldn't save the Apache's life, but it might help ease the pain for a while.

There were other treatments, but no cure. A syrup with different barks, honey, and brandy. Doc Leslie had often suggested drinking a half-pint of thick cream with each meal. But the Apaches weren't likely to have cream in this *ranchería,* and that "gray water" *tizwin* would be a poor substitute for brandy. The outdoor regimen often suggested to consumptives back

East didn't mean wasting away in a round hut high in the mountains in winter with little to eat except horse meat, yucca, and berries.

The old woman mumbled something and squeezed Hannah's hand. *"Gracias,"* she had said in Spanish. *"Vaya con Dios."* Hannah smiled at Nah-dos-te and didn't move until she had drifted back to sleep.

Outside the wickiup, Hannah trembled, and not from the cold. She breathed deeply, wiping her hands and arms with snow, daring not to look back at the wickiup where Nah-dos-te would soon die.

"You help this woman?" Sabana asked.

Hannah shook her head. "I cannot save her. The consumption has spread too far. We can make her comfortable, and no one must go inside that wickiup except you and me." She looked up at the Apache. He nodded.

"This disease can spread," Hannah went on. "It can make all of us sick and die." She thought about Cynthia and the Apache children she had seen playing in camp. They deserved a better fate than to cough themselves to death.

"We will purify ourselves before and after leaving her wickiup," Sabana said. He spoke to himself in his native language, took a deep breath, and told Hannah, "We must fast and pray to *Usen,* the Life Giver."

She told him about the oak bark tea. She figured they were too high up for oaks to grow, but this was Apache land. Sabana or some of the other braves perhaps could travel down the mountains until they found an oak, if there were any in this part of the country. Hannah wasn't sure. She hadn't been looking at trees while riding across New Mexico Territory with Pete or flung over her horse after being captured by Hector.

"Eventually, she'll die, Sabana," Hannah said softly.

The warrior nodded. "This I know. It is bad luck to camp at a place of death, but now we have no choice. Winter will be long."

"Winter will be long," Hannah repeated quietly, looking up as the wet snow fell faster and stung her cheeks. She shook again—this time because of the wind.

The stranger's left arm lifted Pete forward barely two inches, but pain rifled through Belissari's abdomen, causing him to gasp and fill his lungs, which caused even more agony.

"Easy, pardner," the man said. "Let's get a look-see here." His right hand withdrew a Bowie knife, the kind the Confederates used to carry with the brass D-guard, and brought the massive weapon around Pete's back, rested the blade on the arrow shaft near the pine, pressed down, and sawed. A second later, the shaft gave way.

Pete let out a curse. The man laughed as he leaned Pete back. The arrow remained in him, but now he could move.

The mountain man tugged on his long beard. He reminded Pete of Rip van Winkle. Maybe he had been asleep since the War Between the States and had just awakened. Pete could feel blood flowing down his back and stomach. The wound had opened again. He tried to control his breathing, and after a half minute, the man pulled back the oversized coat George the Bouncer had given Pete and studied the arrow.

"Pardner, what do you think?" The accent was Southern, definitely not Texas but maybe Tennessee or the Carolinas. Belissari didn't quite know what his rescuer—or maybe he was simply a tormenter—meant.

A giant left hand rested against Pete's right shoulder while the right clenched the arrow, crushing the feathers. Pete looked into the man's comical eyes. *What's so funny?* he thought.

Belissari swallowed and asked, "What do you mean?" It hurt to speak, and Pete's voice cracked, barely audible.

"Well, do you want me to pull this thing out slooooowly?" He thickened the drawl. "Or you druther me just jerk-the-thing-out-real-quick-like?" He ran the words together as fast as he could. He laughed. "Your choice, pard. Make up your mind."

Pete didn't understand. Well, he was certain of one thing. This old-timer's bedside manners would make Dr. Jack Leslie look like Saint Christopher.

"I—"

"Too late!" the mountain man yelled, and jerked the arrow.

Pete fell forward, screaming, rolling in the snow as pain almost blinded him. He was vaguely aware of the stranger standing beside the Morgan horse, studying the arrow. Pete rested, spread-eagled, gasping. He didn't think he had the energy to move so much.

The man flung the arrow aside, filled his mouth with a fistful of tobacco, and squatted beside Belissari.

"Well, if that didn't kill you, I reckon you might have a chance after all," the mountain man said.

Pete swallowed, summoned up his energy, and began, "You sorry . . ."

But he passed out before he could finish the curse.

Chapter Fourteen

Strange, Hannah thought after Nah-dos-te had passed away, *how cultures differ.* Hannah and Sabana took the old woman's body as far from the camp as they could, and she knew even Sabana feared touching a corpse for so long—and not because Nah-dos-te had died of consumption. He explained that ghosts don't go to the spirit world immediately; they haunt the place where they died. While they were gone, Matitzal and Nah-dos-te's husband burned the dead woman's wickiup.

Hoddentin, her husband, had cried and cut his hair short, and only minutes after Nah-dos-te had breathed her last, Hannah heard the firing of a rifle. It was Hector, shooting about a half-dozen rounds into the air, almost like a military salute. All of the villagers, even the children, took off their clothes and put on rags, despite the bitter cold, and sang songs. Meanwhile, Hannah helped Sabana bathe the old woman's body,

117

dress her in her finest buckskins, and paint her face red. They wrapped the corpse in a robe and left camp.

Nah-dos-te was buried in a small cave, which the two pallbearers covered with snow-covered branches and rocks. Sabana tossed the final limb on the make-shift tomb and said, "Next year may there be many of these trees."

They returned to camp in time to see Matitzal and Hector destroy the rest of the dead woman's belong-ings.

The next day, despite a howling snowstorm, they moved camp. This even surprised Sabana, but he told Hannah it was for the best. One didn't stay in a place of death. They only went about a mile or two. It would have been impossible to go much farther.

Yet the part about Nah-dos-te's death that troubled Hannah the most was the fact that no Apache would ever mention the dead woman's name again. She thought about that as she sewed a new buckskin dress for herself, with help from Hoddentin's other wife. What if she could never say the name of Andrew Les-lie Scott, her father, killed while fighting for the Con-federacy in Virginia in 1865? What if she could never say Rebecca Little Scott, the mother she had never known, the woman who had died giving Hannah life?

And what about these people?

Already one had died. Matitzal's village numbered no more than thirty, with only ten men and maybe three of those younger than forty. The children were sick and cold, half starving, forced to drink corn beer because of wont of food. Even if they survived this winter, these people would never even make it to Colorado, much less Canada.

She remembered her dream. Athena's words came to her again. *"You cannot lead them to Canada. You know that is a mistake. Their place is Mount Ida. This is where they will find peace. You must lead them there."*

"Mount Ida," Hannah said softly.

The middle-aged Apache woman sitting across from her looked up from her awl, bone needle, and sinew, studied Hannah for a second, and asked something in Chiricahua.

Hannah wished she could understand.

Trying to sit up proved to be a major mistake. Belissari sank back down into the warm cot. He was in a log cabin. That much he could tell, covered with a bearskin, his hat and folded wool blanket for a pillow. He pictured Rip van Winkle's face, wondering if he had been dreaming or hallucinating. Well, somebody had moved him inside. Slowly he lifted the bearskin and saw his bandaged abdomen. The wrappings looked strange. After several seconds, he realized they were someone's long underwear.

He dropped the bearskin and drifted back to sleep.

His next bit of half-consciousness involved smells. He caught the aroma of something, something good. His mouth watered. When was the last time he had eaten anything other than snow? Pete opened his eyes, saw the Overlord of Olympus staring back at him, holding a steaming wooden spoon near Belissari's lips. "Take this," white-bearded Zeus commanded.

Pete obeyed the god of earth and air.

A howling coyote brought him out of a deep sleep. Pete cringed. His head felt as if someone had hit him over the head. The miserable, yelping animal sounded as if he were inside the cabin. Slowly, Pete began to understand that this wasn't a coyote. Someone was singing—if you could call it that.

" *'Many are the hearts that are weary tonight/ Wishin' for the war to cease. . . .'* "

Chair legs scraped the wooden floor. A loud sucking came next, then a spitting noise, followed by the ringing of a spittoon. The singer cleared his throat, clapped his hands, began a loud encore:

" *'Tentin' tonight/ Tentin' on the old camp ground!'* Jehoshaphat, pilgrim. You're awake!"

This racket would wake the dead, Pete thought, but he kept quiet. The face appeared. Belissari took a deep breath. Either he remained out of his head, or Rip van Winkle had rescued him. The old man dragged his chair to the cot, sat down, and leaned forward, his jaws working what must have been two pounds of tobacco in his right cheek.

"I found your rifle and revolver, pardner. Cleaned 'em with bear grease and the likes. Reckon I'll have company this winter. My larder ain't no Nashville diner, but we'll make do. Al Sheerar's the name." He held out a weathered right hand.

Mumbling his own name, Pete pulled his arm from under the bearskin and weakly grasped Sheerar's paw.

The mountain man smiled.

"Horse," Pete said weakly. "I left a gray horse in the canyon."

The head, almost hidden by white hair, shook. "Whoever left you to die taken your hoss, pardner. Didn't leave you nothin' but them weapons of your'n, and I found your two pards 'bout twenty rods from you. Deader'n dirt. The Chumley brothers."

Belissari licked his lips. "Not my partners," he said.

"Good. I knowed the Chumleys. Ain't no one gonna cry over their passin'. Now it ain't none of my beeswax, but since you're gonna be eatin' my elk hump and sleepin' on my cot and chewin' my tobaccy, just what the Sam Hill was you doin' up here? Chasin' them Chumleys?"

Pete said no. "Apache," he said. "Kidnapped my . . . my fiancée, and a ten-year-old girl. Been trailin' them since Texas."

Sheerar turned to spray the spittoon with tobacco juice. "Well, that certainly explains that Bedonkohe arrow stickin' through you."

"Bedonkohe?"

The mountain man nodded. "Mogollon Apaches. One of the Eastern bands of the Cherry Cows. Probably tryin' to hook up with that li'l *ranchería* up north of here."

Pete tried to sit up, suddenly excited, wanting to know more, but Sheerar pushed him back down, and Belissari didn't have the strength to resist. "No more talkin', pardner. You'll wear yourself out. You rest. Don't mind my singin' none."

" *'In the prison cell I sit/ Thinkin' Mama, dear, of you. . . .'* "

Alv Sheerar, alias Rip van Winkle, tramped his way across the cabin, clapping his hands like cymbals in the Fort Davis band, singing at the top of his lungs.

"Sleep?" Pete said wearily, but somehow drifted off to peaceful slumber.

The buckskin dress turned out beautifully, heavily fringed, painted blue and yellow, and trimmed with tin cone pendants. Hannah wore it over a cotton shirt and with boot-length elk-skin moccasins, which sadly reminded her of Pete. Could he really still be alive? She wanted to believe that, that the dreams she and Cynthia had were more than just heartfelt wishes.

She felt herself being pulled in opposite directions at night. *Pretend to lead the tribe to Canada. You and Cynthia will have a better chance of escape.* Of course, there was the chance that if the Army caught up with the Apaches, Hector or one of the braves would kill Cynthia and Hannah for spite. *Or tell Matitzal the truth about Sitting Bull, talk him into going to Mexico, safe from the United States Army.* But he wouldn't be safe from the Mexican army, nor scalphunters like the brutal Emilio Vasquez. *Persuade him to surrender, then. It's for the best. They are too few, too weak.* And what chance would they have in some Florida prison, trying to adapt to that climate when they were desert-born? They would die there, too.

Well, she didn't have to make a decision yet. She had all winter to think about it.

The sun had come out, and the snow had stopped.

Hannah sat outside the wickiup watching the children play in the cold. It seemed to be a simple game. They had dug two holes about thirty feet apart, and were throwing stones at a hole. After growing bored with this game, they began racing, boys and girls together, Cynthia among them. The Apache kids were fast, and Cynthia struggled with the snow and her new moccasins. When she finally reached the finish line, a young boy, maybe twelve or fourteen, told Cynthia something in rapid Apache.

"I don't understand," Cynthia said.

The boy repeated. Cynthia shook her head, uncomprehending. So the youth took the girl by her right hand and pulled her across the camp to Sabana, who sat by the fire pit cleaning his rifle. The boy spoke, and Sabana translated for Cynthia. A second later, the girl sprinted across the snow and sat beside Hannah. Panting, the orphan pulled up her dress, loosened and lowered her moccasins, and dipped her hands into a skillet still full of grease from breakfast.

"What in heaven's name are you doing, child?" Hannah asked.

Cynthia excitedly rubbed grease over her calves and thighs. "Feeding my legs, Mama Hannah," she explained. "Napa and Sabana say it'll make me run faster."

Finished, Cynthia pulled up the moccasin tops to her calves, laced them securely, stood, and ran back to the game. The Apache children cheered. Hannah couldn't help but smile. And when the next race began, she stood up and cheered on the ten-year-old. Maybe the grease helped, because Cynthia didn't finish dead last this time. She ran in the middle of the pack, even besting Napa, the boy who had told her to "feed her legs."

Hannah laughed.

Other children congratulated Cynthia on her remarkable improvement. Chest heaving, smiling uncontrollably, Cynthia tried to straighten and said, "That's a fun game, but I got a better one. Y'all know how to play baseball?"

Chapter Fifteen

"Matitzal thinks you should have husband."

Hannah's jaw fell open. She looked at Sabana for a moment, shook her head, and finished cleaning a cut on Napa's left arm, suffered while rough-housing near the horse herd. "Go," she told the boy, and gave him a friendly shove to hurry him along. Hannah looked up at Sabana.

She fingered the necklace she was holding for Cynthia, the one Napa's mother, Mountain Jay In The Juniper, had made for the girl using sinew, turquoise, and rattlesnake rattles.

"Is this the Chiricahua way of proposing?" The Apache warrior didn't understand the sarcasm. Hannah shook her head and asked, "Is the great chief asking me to marry him?"

"No, not Matitzal. He simply think you should have husband to raise *Le'i*. Perhaps Hoddentin. He just lost one wife. Good hunter, Hoddentin. Maybe He Who

Chops Off The Heads Of His Enemies. You have been with him, know he good warrior. Very brave."

"Not Hector," Hannah said bitterly. "Not by a long shot."

Sabana straightened. His eyes turned forceful. "It is not for you to choose. You belong to Matitzal. He decide what best."

Hannah met the Apache's glare and didn't blink until Sabana looked away. Slowly she stood, placed both hands firmly on her hips, and spoke deliberately: "Sabana, hear me well. Bring my message to Matitzal. I will not marry Hector, Hoddentin, nor anybody else in this village. I . . . I have a husband."

"You? You have man?"

"Yes," Hannah said, "and I don't plan on spending all winter fighting off suitors while waiting for him to return."

"Fighting off suitors? This I no understand."

"It's . . . it's from a story my husband told me. Just know that I am married. Tell Matitzal this. Tell him if he wishes me to lead his people to safety, he will not try to force me to marry. He'll rue the day if he does."

"Rue the day? Another story from husband?"

"That's my own. Tell him, Sabana. Tell him now."

The Apache slowly shook his head. *"Besdacada,"* he said. "You were named well."

"I've heard that before."

" 'Away from the home of his love of his love/ Away from his sweetheart or wife. . . .' "

The door swung open, allowing the bitter cold inside, and Alv Sheerar entered the cabin. "Up again, I see, pardner. You're the stubborndest mule these ol' eyes ever laid on."

Steadying himself against the log wall near the stone chimney, Pete turned to smile at the man who had saved his life. Pete had dressed himself in the buckskin pants and shirt Sheerar had left for him. That proved difficult, and pulling on socks and boots almost killed him. But Pete was up now, not dizzy, just tired. He held the coat George the Bouncer had given him.

"Goin' somewheres?" the mountain man asked, pointing the barrel of his Sharps rifle at the coat.

Belissari nodded. "I was just waiting to thank you and tell you goodbye. I've got to find those Apaches."

With a nod, Sheerar leaned the big rifle in a corner. "Well, can't blame you none there. But you ain't goin' anyplace, pard, not till morn. Another good night's sleep'll do you good. Them Cherry Cows ain't goin' nowheres nohow. 'Sides, I'm cookin' up a treat. It ain't no Brunswick stew, but my belly says it'll fill the bill any day of the week. Sit down, pardner. Warm yourself some more. You gotta admit, I build one cozy cabin and a mean fireplace."

Pete didn't argue. He found an unsteady chair as Sheerar busied himself around the cabin, brought Pete a cup of coffee, and tossed the horseman's coat on the cot. "That there coat of yourn," Alv said, "likely saved you from frostbite. Them sleeves is so long, they covered your hands, protected you a mite. Now, I warrant had I been a day later, you'd be in much poorer shape, pard. Likely, I'd have to bury you come spring when the ground's thawed."

Supper was stew, sourdough biscuits, coffee, and, because Pete was leaving the next morning, two fingers of rye whiskey. "Got to ration the bug juice," Alv told Pete. "I had to feed you a couple of my bottles when you was half out of your noggin."

"Thanks," Pete said. The whiskey went down easily. Belissari had expected it to be rotgut from Hades. "I can't repay you for everything you've done, and I hate to ask another favor."

Sheerar laughed. "Lemme guess. You want a hoss."

Pete nodded. The mountain man slapped both thighs. "I knowed it. Ain't much hope of you catchin' up with that lady gal of yourn without a hoss to ride. Well, Alv Sheerar must be your guardian angel, pard, because it just so happens that I got me a piebald nag I can loan out to you. Miserable ol' mare, but you can ride 'er. Don't even have to bring her back when you're finished. It's Alvin Hans Sheerar's gift to his first pard since 18 and 79. I had to shoot that rapscallion dead."

Belissari fell silent and returned to eating.

"So," Sheerar said, "you taken a likin' to my woodrat stew."

Alv Sheerar didn't do such a great job rationing his liquor. As soon as they had finished eating—and Pete stopped shortly after hearing the ingredients—the oldtimer topped Belissari's coffee cup, then chugged down a healthy portion of the rest of the bottle. Tobacco juice might have often dribbled down Sheerar's whiskers, but he was careful not to lose any whiskey.

"Ahhhhh." The big man wiped the mouth behind all of that hair with the back of his hand.

Belissari took another sip of rye.

"What brings you to these mountains, Alv?" Pete asked. He knew nothing of Sheerar except that the man couldn't carry a tune and shouted his songs more than sang them.

"Glad you asked that, pardner. Mighty glad." Sheerar took another pull of rye, smacked his lips, and lit into another song. " *'Hoo-rah! Hoo-rah! For Southern rights hoo-rah!'* "

Another drink. Only four fingers of rye remained.

"You recollect that ol' song, pardner?" Without waiting for Pete's reply, the man continued. "We sang it durin' the war." He smacked his lips, studied the bottle, and decided to ration for a few minutes. "That's the War of Northern Aggression. You ain't no Yank, is you, pard?"

"Born in Texas."

"Texas! Glory to Texas. Glory to John Bell Hood! Did you wear the gray? Nah. 'Course not. You're too young to have fit the Yanks. But not me. No sir. Not Alvin Hans Sheerar. First sergeant I was. Signed up in Memphis with the best man that ever forked a saddle, raised a saber, and popped a cap against those bluebellies." He raised the bottle. "To Gen'ral Bedford Forrest!"

Bottle and coffee cup clinked. Sheerar drained the rye and picked up his story.

" 'Course, I had seen the elephant before. I fit the Mexicans with Gen'ral Taylor, I did. Left Auntie Alifair's farm in Greene County when I was sixteen.

Maybe younger, maybe older. It's been a spell. Well, I stayed down in your neck of the woods, Texas, a tad after that war. And then I catched the fever. Gold. Off I went to California. Didn't see enough color to fill a tooth. I taken off for Colorado up 'round Denver City, then started driftin' I did. Freighted some in Kansas but didn't take a likin' to that country like it was, flatter'n the brim of a Boss of the Plains. Wed me a gal down in the Ozarks in Arkansas, Lill Beeber her name was, afore she throwed me out. Worked on the riverboats in St. Louis and Memphis. And then the war broken out, I joined up again.

"Now if you can tell me how it was that we lost that li'l set-to, I'd surely like to know. Best fightin' men I ever seen wore the gray. Gen'ral Forrest. Gen'ral Hood. But you knowed the story, bein' Texan and all. The bluebellies won the war, but they never got me to say no oath of allegiance. No sir. Not me. I heard that Jo Shelby was aimin' to take us Rebs down to Mexico, so I lit a shuck for south of the border. Never did see ol' Shelby, and I covered a lot of that country. Fought for that French gent for a while, then I decided to help them Mexicans out. And then . . ."

His eyes twinkled. Sheerar pulled out his tobacco pouch and stuffed his mouth before continuing.

"You guessed it, pardner. I catched the fever once more. Went up north, back to the United States of America and the territories. Struck a fortune up north of here near Wheeler Peak and lost it the next day." His laughter shook the rough-hewn table, maybe even the entire cabin. "That's the way it is, pardner, with gold. Next I was back in Colorado. Shot buffalo for one of the railroad crews up north of there. Or maybe that was later. I disremember. But I got all the way to Montana Territory one time and got me a silver mine, I did. Gospel truth. Sold it and bought me a ranch down Arizona way.

"Ranchin' ain't for me, pard. I got out of that business in less'n a year, headed back north. Black Hills. Sioux country. Did I tell you I met Gen'ral Custer once? Well, I did. Afore he lost his hair to them Sioux and Cheyenne, of course. Yep, I met that dumb Yankee blowhard. Got what he deserved he did. So where does that bring me to?"

Pete sipped his rye. "1876."

"Seventy and six. Yep. That sounds 'bout right. Well, I must have made me another fortune because I don't remember nothin' till September of '79 when I partnered with Dutch Larry Langendorf up on the Medicine Bow. I dissolved that there partnership—*dissolved*: I learned that word at my trial in Laramie— when I caught him a-stealin' from me. Jury didn't believe me and they sent me to the Big House, but I got tired of that place and me and Bo Atkinson escaped on Christmas Eve 18 and 80.

"Well, I went south. Bo headed up to Virginia City—the Montana burg, not the one in Nevada, never been there—and got hisself hunged for murderin' a card shark. I tried Tombstone in Arizona for a spell, but longed for the high country. Spent a couple years in the Rockies in Colorado, came back down here, freighted for a spell in Mexico, panned for some color in the Sierra Madres, and then got a hankerin' to try my luck up here. Here I be. And I bet you're one mighty glad pilgrim that I didn't elect to spend a longer spell down in Mexico.

"Am I right, pardner?"

Belissari raised his glass in a toast and smiled. Sheerar spit, missed the spittoon because he was laughing so hard, and didn't care.

" *'Away, away, away down south in Dixie....'* "

Sheerar let loose with a Johnny Reb cry. Belissari groaned and pulled himself, fully dressed, out of the cot. "Hello, pardner," the sadistic rescuer said. "You all rested and ready?"

Pete replied and pulled his coat on. He knew he was pushing himself. He could use another week in bed. Outside, the wind howled. It wasn't the best time to travel, weak as he was, but he had to get to Hannah and Cynthia. After buckling on his gunbelt and grabbing his rifle, he shook Alv Sheerar's meaty paw.

"You dead set on travelin', pard?"

"I'm afraid so."

"Well, I was hopin' you might winter with me. I got a book someone given me one time, but I never learned my letters. But I can play some cards—that's why I lost so many fortunes. Figured we might pass a few months playin' five-card stud or draw poker, and maybe, iff'n you can read, you could tell me what that book be about. What's your favorite card game, pardner?"

Belissari smiled. "I never was much good at cards, Alv."

The old man sat at the table, shaking his head.

"Well, I wish you luck. You'll find the piebald and a rig in the barn. Texas rig. The Denver saddle's mine. Best of luck to you, pardner."

They shook hands again.

Anticipating the cold, Pete pulled up his bandanna before opening the door. Behind him, Alv Sheerar had produced a deck of cards and began to shuffle them. Belissari raised the latch, swung the door open, and stepped outside into a world of gray and white.

This he hadn't expected.

A biting wind drove giant, wet flakes to the ground. Already the snow rested waist-deep. He could make out a path Sheerar must have dug. Belissari could only guess it led to the barn or woodpile because he could see no more than an arm's length, and the path was filling up fast. The wind cut like ice. Belissari stepped back inside, numb, and closed the door.

"Hee hee hee." Sheerar's snickers turned into cackles, then a hearty roar.

Pete pulled down his bandanna, leaned the Bullard repeater against the wall, and faced the mountain man.

"Stud or draw poker, pardner?" Sheerar asked, and began to deal without waiting for an answer.

Chapter Sixteen

Alv Sheerar bawled like a newborn calf the first time Porthos died. But by the time Pete made it through *The Man in the Iron Mask* a third time and told how the king's heroic musketeer was sleeping the eternal sleep, the mountain man had a better handle on his emotions and merely sobbed quietly as Pete read and turned the page. Belissari, on the other hand, had sickened of Athos, Aramis, D'Artagnan, King Louis, and all of France, including the novel's noted author, Alexandre Dumas.

Pete had found himself in a routine. Up in the morning, stoke the fire, dress, make his way through the snow to the barn, break ice so the piebald and Morgan could drink, feed the horses, grab an armload of wood, return to the cabin, and make breakfast. Wearing crudely fashioned snowshoes, Alv Sheerar would disappear later that morning on a hunt or scout or to check his traps, and Pete would split wood. Swinging the ax strengthened him. No longer did his stomach hurt. In fact, Belissari felt better now than he had in maybe years.

Well, he itched considerably. He needed a bath. He longed to brush his teeth. His beard scratched, and his tangled, long hair needed a brush and curry comb. The buckskins he wore were filthy. Pete's hands were grimy. He had no idea how his face looked. His host owned an old copy of a French novel, translated into English, that had been rained on a few times and was missing about a half-dozen pages, but Alv Sheerar had no mirror.

"Good, clean mountain livin'," the old-timer often said. "Does the body a world of good."

Clean, Pete said to himself, *might be an over-statement.*

Afternoons were spent on other chores, preparing supper, checking on the stock, mending tack and making other repairs, replenishing the sourdough starter, bringing in enough firewood to last the night, and playing cards. Five-card stud. Five-card draw. Seven-card stud. They used coffee beans for chips. After supper, before it got too dark, Pete would open *The Man in the Iron Mask* and read aloud. Then he'd go to bed and listen to Sheerar's stories.

His murder trial in Laramie.

Fighting the Yanks with Nathan Bedford Forrest.

Life near Sutter's Mill in California.

Stealing, or rather "borrowin' some John Barley-corn," from his uncle's still in Greene County.

Killing his first bear in Tennessee.

Running from the Apache Nana in '81.

Running from his wife in Boone County, Arkansas.

Searching for gold in the Sierra Madres.

Breaking out of the Wyoming state penitentiary.

Suffering from dysentery during the Mexican War.

It added up to more information that Pete wanted to know, but he liked Alv Sheerar, and not only because the man had saved his life. Sure, he could talk all night and half the next morning and break into a loud Johnny Reb song at any second, but he was friendly, a good man at heart. In a way, Pete would hate to leave him when the snow began to melt.

Belissari looked up from the book. "You all right, Alv?"

Sheerar blew his nose. "Yeah, pardner. Sure. Go on. We gots time for one more chapter."

" 'Chapter Seventy-nine,' " Pete read. " 'The Epitaph of Porthos.' "

The mountain man failed to stifle a low moan.

It wasn't exactly spring in the high country, but Matitzal announced one sunny morning that the time had come to break winter camp and continue their journey to Grandmother's Country. No one smiled, although Hannah knew everyone was glad to be moving to lower elevations. The Apaches usually made winter camp in the desert, but Matitzal had chosen the high mountains to stay hidden from the whites. Hannah couldn't fault that reasoning, although it had taken a toll on his people. Hannah herself had probably lost close to fifteen pounds that winter. Some of the old men and women were emaciated, reminding her of the late Nah-dos-te, who had wasted away from consumption.

As the villagers began preparations for a long journey, Hector, Sabana, and Matitzal approached Hannah. *"Besdacada,"* Sabana said. "Matitzal ask questions about journey."

She nodded. The four went inside the chief's wickiup and sat in a circle. The three men smoked the pipe before the humpbacked leader grunted and spoke in Chiricahua.

Sabana translated: "How far is it to this Grandmother's Country?"

Hannah had no idea. A thousand miles? Two thousand? "Many sleeps," she finally answered. "Many moons. A difficult, long journey. Some may not survive."

This brought about an animated discussion between the three Apaches. As they talked, Hannah suddenly understood the reason no one had smiled when Matitzal announced his decision to leave for Canada. They didn't want to go north. They wanted to live in their homeland. Of course, that was impossible, except on reservations, and it seemed that the people of Arizona were determined to rid the entire territory of the Apaches. Here in New Mexico? The Mescaleros had a reservation southeast of here, but if Matitzal's people were to surrender, Hannah knew they would join the other Chiricahuas in the swampy prisons back East.

Yet they couldn't hide forever in the mountains. But what of Mexico? The Apache range stretched far south of the border. The climate, she could only guess, would be better than the harsh winter they had just survived. Mexico was bigger, less populated. If bandits and revolutionaries could hide in those desert mountains, why not thirty Bedonkohe Apaches?

She looked back at the men. Sabana was speaking to her. He repeated the question. "Do you know of this Sitting Bull of the Lakota?"

Hannah swallowed. "I have never met him. Have never seen him. I hear he is a great leader among the Sioux, the way Matitzal is a great leader among his people." Over the winter, she had learned all about flattery, all about communicating with the Apaches, especially men such as Matitzal. Hector glared at her. He understood English—and without a doubt, he recognized her motives.

The Apache chief smiled as Sabana relayed Hannah's words.

North, Hannah though, *toward Canada.* They would never get there, not even close. South to Mexico, they had a slim chance if they could dodge Army patrols and the like. But if Hannah led them to Mexico, what were the chances that she and Cynthia would ever be free? Matitzal promised Hannah a reward for leading them to Sitting Bull. He had said nothing of Mexico, and Hannah knew the Apaches hated the Mexicans.

Outside, the wind began to moan. Hannah thought she could hear Athena's words again. *"You cannot lead them to Canada. Their place is Mount Ida."*

Matitzal had begun another speech, a long, rambling story that bored his son. When he fell silent, Sabana spoke:

"Once, Earth was new. This before time of White Eyes. Even before time of my grandfather's grandfather. Before Coyote brought Death to the world. Yet many people no live right. Anger *Usen*, the Life Giver. So *Usen* cause great flood that cover land of the Bedonkohe and all land of The People. None of The People survive this great flood."

A great flood, Hannah thought, and remembered the story of Noah from the Bible. Strange but wonderful how whites and Apaches were so different yet shared some beliefs. Sabana continued.

"Only lone rooster survived this flood. It floated on piece of cottonwood. All rooster saw was water. *Usen* had covered all of world with water, except one spot. A white mountain in land of The People was not covered. Only top of mountain sticks out, but rooster see it and drift to land. Rooster is alone for many moons as water seeps back into land.

"After that, Child of the Water and White Painted Woman come. They create human beings again, and many Bedonkohe. Since that time, The People live in this country. This our homeland. It difficult to leave. But is easy to die. It hard to live. Stay here, The People die. In Grandmother's Country, we live. *Tatanka-Iyotanka* will help. Must help. He is not of The People, but he no White Eye. This why we leave here. You guide us."

"No."

The word shot out of Hannah's mouth before she could think. Snarling, Hector put his right hand on his knife. For once, Matitzal's face registered shock. He understood *no,* understood Hannah's sharp tone. Sabana's face turned rock solid.

Hannah took a deep breath, exhaled slowly, looked Matitzal in those dark eyes.

"There is a story that I must tell," she said evenly.

"You got the cipherin' done, pardner?"

Pete took a pencil to the frontispiece of *The Man in the Iron Mask*. He struck through a number, jabbed the point down, smiled, and tugged on his uneven beard before looking up.

"The way I see it," Belissari began, "I owe you twenty-one thousand, forty-four dollars in five-card draw. But I took you for nineteen thousand, eight hundred and seventy-nine in five-card stud. You won three hundred and ten dollars off me in seven-card stud—"

"I had you in the hole a lot worser than that, pard, but you had a good run last week," Sheerar interrupted.

"That's right. But I fed the horses for you twice, at two hundred dollars a pop, plus I checked the traps for you yesterday at another five hundred—"

"Don't forget that you sold me your last cup of bug juice, too."

Pete laughed. "I'm not about to forget that, Alv. That was for one thousand dollars."

"So, what's it all come out to?"

"You owe me four hundred and twenty-five dollars."

"Great Jehoshaphat, pardner. I'll be a suck-egg mule. That don't likely seem worth the effort, only four hundred bucks."

"You're right. Let's just say I'll buy that piebald and rig from you and we'll call it even."

"No, sir! Not on your life. I given that hoss and outfit to you. I ain't no welsher."

"All right, then you buy me a beer and a whiskey sometime."

"Done!"

They clasped hands.

"I reckon this is adiós, eh, pardner?"

"Reckon so, Alv. Take care of yourself."

In the barn, Belissari brushed and combed the piebald before throwing on a saddle blanket and the Texas rig. Sheerar had been wrong about the mare. She was no nag. Broad hindquarters, powerful legs, muscular neck, standing about fourteen and a half hands, with white legs and a predominantly black body, the mare had grown to trust Pete over the course of the winter. The pinto was lean now, but she'd fatten up. Like a lot of Texans, Pete had never cared much for paint horses, but Milady—he had named her after Dumas's villainness in *The Three Musketeers*; it beat Sheerar's "ol' piebald gluebait"—would carry him across these mountains. He placed the top of the bridle on the piebald's white face, pressed his right thumb into the corner of the horse's mouth, slipped in the bit, and pulled the top over the mare's ears.

"We're going to get along just fine, Milady," he said as he tightened the saddle cinch and found the breast collar. The mare snickered and pricked her ears forward. Pete looked up and heard the crunching of boots in snow.

" *'I catched the rheumatism/ From campin' in the snow. . . .' "*

"Hello, pardner!" Alv Sheerar grabbed his saddle and blanket and walked to the big Morgan. "I elected to come along with you."

Pete rose slowly. "Alv," he said. "There's no need for that. This is dangerous. I don't want you getting hurt on my account."

"Pardner. Now I ain't gonna argue with you none. If the Union and Mexican armies couldn't hurt ol' Alvin Hans Sheerar, then ain't no worn-out Cherry Cows gonna make me cry for mommy."

"Hector is no worn-out Chiricahua."

"Don't scare me none. 'Sides, what was that you said them Frenchie musketeers said? 'All for one, and one for all'?"

"Alv, you've got no reason—"

"Sure I do. We's pards, ain't we?"

Pete shook his head. He was getting nowhere. Pardner this. Pardner that. "Pards?" he finally tried in desperation. "Alv, we've wintered together for three months and you don't even know my name."

"Sure I do, pardner. Your name . . . your name's Jim. Now tighten that cinch, pilgrim. Else you'll be eatin' a pound of snow and mud when he go down this ol' knob."

Chapter Seventeen

"You have heard the story of the Little Bighorn," Hannah said, trying to hide her nerves, "when Sitting Bull and the Lakota wiped out Custer of the bluecoats and his men?"

"*Sí,*" Sabana replied before explaining to Matitzal. The grizzled chief nodded. Hector still looked angry.

"After this great victory, Sitting Bull led his people north to Grandmother's Country, what we call Canada, to escape the wrath of the White Eyes. The Bedonkohe know too well this wrath." She paused, allowing Sabana to translate, took another deep breath, let the air out slowly, and resumed her speech.

"The Lakota stayed in Grandmother's Country for many moons"—how long, she couldn't remember—"and there was peace. Soldiers of Canada are not as ruthless as soldiers of my people. But living there . . . away from their true homeland . . . this proved false in the hearts of the Lakota." She was stretching things

143

now, perhaps. All she really remembered about Sitting Bull's exile in Canada was that he went up there, stayed a while, then came back to surrender and be pinned on a reservation. But it sounded true. It was how she would have felt.

"They longed to go home, to be with their people they had left behind. So Sitting Bull left Grandmother's Country and returned to his homeland, to surrender to the White Eyes. He has been living on a reservation since. There is nothing for the Bedonkohe in Grandmother's Country. Sitting Bull cannot help you. Even if you make it to this country, The People will die. Winters there are longer and colder than what we just went through." That had to be true. Her friend Buddy Pecos told her once that the snow in Wyoming hit you like a fist, so it had to be worse in Canada. "Bluecoats will block the path to Grandmother's Country with many guns. If the great Matitzal leads his people north, he leads them to death."

Matitzal frowned as the words reached his ears. Hector drew his knife and said, in dry English, "You lie."

Hannah stood firm. "You know I tell the truth, Hector. You lived with the soldiers long enough to know that the last free Indians are the Apaches. That is why you want to go to Canada. You would rather die fighting for freedom than submit. You would rather be remembered as a warrior. You would rather see your father die at the hands of soldiers."

Matitzal turned to his son. He spoke in Chiricahua. At first Hector did not answer, but the chief raised his voice. His son turned angrily, shouted at the old man and stormed out of the wickiup.

The old Apache's head dropped. His words came quietly, almost broken. Sabana softly translated: "You speak truth. Matitzal has heavy heart. We no go to Grandmother's Country. We submit to White Eyes, go to this Flo-ri-da."

The wickiup fell silent. Tears welled in Hannah's eyes. She brushed one off her cheeks. "Sabana," she said after a minute. "Tell Matitzal there is another choice ... Mexico. It is closer. You can hide out there." She knew she would have to sell the weary leader on the idea, and to do that she had to be honest.

"When I first arrived at the *ranchería* of your people, on the first night I slept in the wickiup of the great Matitzal, a vision came to me. A goddess of ... of my husband's people ... spoke these words. Know that I tell you the truth, Matitzal. This vision has troubled me all winter. I thought it might be false. But Le'i had a similar vision the same night. The goddess said that I should not lead the Bedonkohe to Grandmother's Country. She told me that only death awaits The People there. I should lead them to another place, a place called Mount Ida. This I think would have to be in Mexico. Please do not surrender to the soldiers. I fear that death also awaits The People in Florida."

Matitzal answered and left the hut. Sabana told Hannah: "Matitzal never heard of this Mount Ida. He know *Besdacada* speak from heart, not falsely. Now Matitzal must find cave and hope his spirit tell him what he should do. We wait."

* * *

Three days passed. Hannah began to fear that Matitzal had died, but one morning a cry ran through the camp and she recognized the humpbacked chief stumble through the slushy snow and stand in front of the fire pit as the villagers gathered around. Hannah put her arm around Cynthia and joined the crowd.

He raised his lance over his head and spoke, making eye contact with everyone, even Hannah and Cynthia. Hannah saw the excited looks on the nearby faces, even thought she glimpsed a smile or two. The people cheered when Matitzal finished and lowered his spear. Two women broke into a song. She felt Sabana standing beside her. The warrior whispered, "Matitzal say we try this Mexico. It is land of Bedonkohe. His guide, the antelope, come to him and tell what we must do. We return to land where The People reborn. Land where rooster saved after flood. This holy mountain. There is white ring where high water reached, this at top of mountain. Matitzal no know where to find this mountain. It long forgotten among The People. But *Besdacada* has strong vision. You . . . you will lead us to this place. You can find this white-ringed mountain. This is what Matitzal tell The People. We leave at first light. You lead us."

Hannah stared ahead without seeing anything. She was vaguely aware that Sabana had left, knew she stood with Cynthia, realized the girl was staring up, fingering her Apache necklace, waiting for some sort of acknowledgement if only a smile to let her know that Hannah knew what she was doing. Hannah gripped Cynthia's right shoulder. "Go on, Cynthia. Get your stuff together. We've got a long trip ahead of us."

"Yes, Mama Hannah."

Hannah stared at the fire, breathed in the smoke. She had been in Mexico before, but barely across the Rio Grande. She definitely wasn't qualified to be a guide, but she had talked an Apache chief into trusting his life—and the lives of twenty-nine other Indians— with her. *Oh, what have I done?* she prayed silently.

"A white-ringed mountain," Hannah said aloud, still staring at the flames.

"Mount Ida."

His boots sank deep into the mud as he swung from Milady. He had long forgotten about the broken foot suffered back in Texas. Even the arrow wound seemed a distant memory. Pete knelt, holding the reins in his gloved left hand. He gripped the elkskin fingertips on his right hand with his teeth and pulled off the other glove before testing the ashes in the fire pit.

Warm. A day old. Two at the most. He felt excited. They were close. How fast could an Apache village travel in this country? He pulled himself stiffly into the saddle with a grunt. Out of practice, he thought. He hadn't been on a horse that winter. Buddy Pecos would laugh at this. Pete Belissari, the great mustanger, having trouble getting on a horse. His legs and backside would toughen up quickly. The second day was usually the worst. In a day or two, he would be his old self again.

Belissari kicked the piebald and followed the trail.

He heard the voice long before he rode up to Alv Sheerar.

"*'The ol' church bell will ring with joy/ Hoo-rah! Hoo-rah!. . . .'*"

The song died before Pete rounded a bend and saw Sheerar sitting on a stump, smoking a pipe, Sharps rifle cradled across his lap, looking like Rip van Winkle once more. The mountain man tapped the corncob pipe on the stump and took another long pull before standing.

"Might not be too good an idea to go about singing, Alv," Pete suggested.

Sheerar waved off Belissari's concerns. "Bosh. If them Apaches can hear me, they'll think I'm a-singin' my war song. It'll scare 'em, pardner. I been waitin' for you. Got somethin' you oughta see."

He stuck the pipe in his coat pocket, grabbed the reins to the Morgan and walked a few rods before kneeling and fingering what appeared to be a hoof print. Belissari dropped from the saddle, loose-reined Milady, and squatted beside his partner. The print came from a shod horse.

"We ain't the only ones a-trailin' them Cherry Cows, pilgrim," Sheerar said flatly.

Frowning, Pete studied the sign. He wanted to believe this horse was part of the Apache herd. Hector had stolen plenty of horses—including Poseidon—and they all would be wearing metal shoes. But this wasn't part of the trail. This man was riding alone, off to the side because the path of the Apaches was easy to follow.

"Whoever it be, he ain't in no particular hurry,

pard," Sheerar said. "I followed his trail a spell, and 'bout a half-mile downhill he swung off that-away like he's makin' a wide loop 'round them Cherry Cows." Sheerar guided his left foot into the stirrup and with a grunt pulled his behemoth frame into the saddle. The Morgan snorted under the mountain man's weight.

"Could be he figured out he was followin' some Apaches and got scared. That'd be the smart thing to do."

"Could be," Pete said uneasily, and mounted the pinto mare. He kicked the horse into a walk and pulled up alongside Sheerar as they rode down the mountain trail.

"You wanna hear my guess, pard?" As usual, Sheerar didn't wait to continue. "Ain't nobody up in these mountains this time of year without no reason. Might be on the owlhoot, but I ain't a-bettin' on that. No sir. I say that gent knows he's trailin' some Cherry Cows. He followed 'em to get a good idea as to wheres they's headin', and now he's gone to head 'em off. Speakin' of which, I thought you said them Apaches was headin' north?"

"They were." Pete studied the old man's theory. He knew Sheerar was right.

"Well, they ain't goin' that-away no more. You can makes a clear path north all the way to the Rio Salado iff'n you wants to. And if I was an Apache on the run, that's how I'd do it, yes sir, I surely would. Nope, these Cherry Cows done changed their direction. They's headin' south."

"So it seems." Pete wasn't in a talkative mood.

Sheerar reined in his horse. Pete did the same. The

mountain man pointed to his left, indicating another trail. "That's where our new friend rode off. Quicker way into the low country. Now, pardner, you got any idea who this gent might be?"

Belissari nodded, but he didn't want to say. He hoped he was wrong.

He knew he was right.

"Emilio Vasquez," he answered. "A scalphunter."

Sheerar grunted, reached inside his coat, and pulled out his tobacco pouch. "Last of my chaw," he complained, and worked the plug for half a minute before speaking again. He let the Morgan lower its head to scrounge for forage. Pete did the same.

After spitting out a tobacco stem, the old-timer stroked his thick beard and said, "Scalphunter, you say. Never had no use for that breed. Ain't never heard of this Vasquez, but I already taken a dislikin' to the gent. I suspect you have, too."

"It's personal," Pete said.

"I knowed that feelin', pard."

Belissari felt thirsty. He reached for his canteen, took a few swallows, but didn't feel much better. "Vasquez is evil. He butchered his own people, Mexicans."

Sheerar let out a curse. "Well, then I'd be a-bettin' that this Vasquez aims to ambush them Apaches. Might get some help. That don't likely mean nothin' good for your gal, pard. If this fellow is as bad as you say he is, he'll murder her, too, and the li'l one."

Belissari could only nod.

"Then here's my plan, pardner. I'm gonna follow this scalphunter's trail. You follow them Cherry Cows.

If I catch up with the man first, I'll kill 'im. Meantime, maybe you can get them girls free from those Apaches. And if the scalphunter reaches the Apaches first, well, then I'll be behind him. Might be we could get him in a crossfire. How's that sound?"

"Sounds good," Pete said. They shook hands.

"Good luck, Alv."

"Luck yourself, Jim."

Chapter Eighteen

They had camped that night in a meadow, stuffing themselves with meat from a black bear Hector had killed. As dawn broke, the villagers began preparations to resume their journey, loading goods on travois pulled by dogs and horses. Hannah rubbed her aching feet before pulling on the moccasins. Apaches could travel all day on foot. Hannah preferred on the back of a horse in a comfortable saddle made by rancher and neighbor Julian Cale's best vaquero. She bit off a piece of venison jerky for breakfast and gave the rest to Cynthia.

The gunshot ripped sharply through the cold, morning air, echoing across the meadow. Hannah jumped up.

Gripping his stomach with both hands, weaving as though he were drunk on *tizwin,* Hoddentin staggered toward her. Horses shied from him. People talked excitedly, confused. Only Matitzal and Hector seemed to realize what was happening. The old chief ran to Hoddentin and put his arm around the man's shoulders, knocking off the wounded man's red cotton headband. Agony masked Hoddentin's face. He let out a low moan and uncupped his hands around his abdomen.

Cynthia gasped. Glistening crimson stained the warrior's yellow shirt. He dropped to his knees, pulling Matitzal to the ground with him.

Apaches had no death song. Hannah had learned that during her stay. Hoddentin mumbled something and pitched forward, facedown in the mud. Matitzal raised both hands over his head, fists clenched, and let out a beastly howl.

Another shot boomed. A horse screamed, kicked and died.

Apaches wailed. A dog took off across the meadow, spilling the contents of the travois as he loped madly in terror. Napa, the boy Cynthia had befriended, fell behind the dead horse and covered his ears. He began to cry.

A bullet splintered a piece of wood near the fire. Another whined off a rock.

Hannah heard another roar. She turned and saw Hector draw his knife and sprint toward her and Cynthia. Another gunshot. There stood Sabana, trying to control a rearing horse. He was yelling something. Somehow, Hannah made out his words.

"Run, *Besdacada!* He means to kill you and *Le'i!*"

She understood, turned, shoved Cynthia. "Run, Cynthia!" Hannah shouted and pushed the girl forward, hard. "Run as fast as you have ever run! Go!"

The girl sprang into the forest. Hannah went the

other way, not as fast at first, waiting to make sure
Hector followed her. He did. She dodged a horse,
stepped over an overturned brass kettle, pulled up her
dress and ran into the meadow. Hector screamed savagely in Apache and followed.

A pine cone dug into her left heel. She grimaced
and continued, fighting for breath. A bullet whistled
past her head. Was the shooter aiming for her or Hector? She felt the Apache gaining, so she cut left, then
right, sprinted for the forest. Mistake. She slipped on
a patch of snow, slid into the grass and mud. Her lungs
hurt. Hector sailed over her. He had tripped, too.

She sprang up, filled her lungs, stumbled, and made
her way back to the Apache camp. Another gunshot.

Why is Hector after me?

Scenes ran together. Napa crying. Matitzal screaming with furry. Terrified faces. A horse rearing, crash-
ing to the ground. She dodged Hoddentin's other wife,
already chopping off her hair, tears streaming down
her leathery, copper face. A man, a boy actually, trying
to pull her away from her husband's body, to the forest, out of the line of fire. Another shot. A woman
screamed.

Hannah turned right, heading toward the mountain
trail they had come down yesterday, purposely taking
the opposite direction Cynthia had gone. Hector closed
in again. She heard him panting. She could picture him
behind her, knife raised, reaching out, screaming in
Apache.

She screamed.

His hand fell between her shoulder blades, pushing.
No balance. Hannah flew forward. A small stone dug

into her ribs. Air exploded from her lungs. Her vision
blurred. A shot rang out. She rolled over. No. Someone rolled her over. Hector straddled her, raised the
knife. He shouted again. The black eyes locked on
Hannah.

"Trickster!" he said in English. "Like Coyote. Trap
us. Now, Hector kills you!"

Pete heard the shot. Sheerar? Vasquez? Somebody
else? Another round echoed. He swore, drew the Bullard from the scabbard, jacked in a fresh shell and put
Milady into a gallop.

He ducked beneath the limbs, saw the clearing
ahead of him. An Apache brave pushed a skinny Indian woman to the ground, jumped on top of her,
raised his knife, and shouted something. Apache
woman? She had blond hair, though it was dirty and
greasy. Hannah? Pete put the reins in his teeth,
brought the rifle stock to his shoulder, steadied the
barrel as best he could with both hands as the mare
surged forward.

Don't shoot, he told himself. *You might hit Hannah.*

He swore, pitched the rifle aside and, dived from
the saddle.

The Apache—*By Zeus, it's Hector!*—looked up and
tried to stand. Pete's shoulder crashed into the man's
chest. White pain flashed. He tasted grass and mud.
Belissari struggled for breath, climbed to his knees in
a hurry, looked left, right, saw Hector reaching for the
knife.

Pete stood, ready.

Hector charged, and feinted left. The blade slashed.

Hannah sat up, trying to figure out what had just happened. Some crazy man in buckskins had tackled Hector. They were fighting. The long-haired, bearded stranger dodged a vicious swipe of the knife, backing up, fists raised, on the defensive.

Her lips trembled.

Could it be . . .

The man let out a curse, swung at Hector, missed, dodged the blade again. She recognized the voice.

Pete!

The gunshots had stopped. Why? It couldn't have been Pete shooting at them, Hannah thought. Could it? No. Hannah stood. The Apaches had taken cover in the forest, holding horses and young ones, watching the fight in the meadow. Hoddentin's body remained where he had fallen. Two women helped another woman, shot, it seemed. Where was Matitzal? She searched the trees, finally spotted him, watching his son and Pete locked in battle. Sabana stood nearby. Matitzal spoke and Sabana raised his rifle.

Hannah yelled. She scrambled to her feet and ran to the men. "No!" she yelled, and repeated the words she had learned in Apache. *"No. It is my husband!"*

Sabana hesitated. Matitzal studied Hannah for a moment, then considered his son. His right arm pushed down the barrel of Sabana's breechloader. He spoke quietly in Apache. Sabana nodded, said something to another warrior, and they disappeared, heading, Hannah guessed, to find the man who had ambushed them.

Hannah focused her attention on Pete.

*   *   *

Panting, Belissari backed up, eyes following the knife Hector wielded. The brave smiled savagely, enjoying this. Pete tired of this, and reached for the holstered Colt. Fear replaced Hector's smile. He charged. Pete had the revolver halfway out when he tripped. He landed with a thud, legs draped over a dead Indian's body. Hector's right moccasin kicked out, stinging Pete's hand. The revolver flew away. Hector changed his grip on the knife and brought the blade down with a killing thrust.

Belissari rolled left. The blade dug into the meadow. Hector grunted. Pete sprang up, kicked back at the Apache. His boot crunched against the warrior's jaw. The Indian fell backward, lost the hold of his knife. Pete saw the glimmer of the blade as it sank into wet grass. He reached . . .

Hector tackled him. They separated somehow. Pete lay on his back, saw the Indian recover and charge again. Quickly, Belissari brought his knees up, kicked forward, his boots catching Hector in the stomach. Pete rocked on his back and saw Hector cartwheel overhead, land hard again, and almost immediately scramble to his feet.

Belissari swore again and stood. *Doesn't anything stop this guy?*

They circled each other. Time for another tactic. Pete feinted with a left, then swung his right fist hard. Indians, he had heard, weren't used to fistfights or boxing. Of course, Belissari was far from a champion pugilist. Hector blocked the blow and came up hard with a haymaker left that split Pete's lips. He backed up, stunned, and spit out blood. So much for that theory. Hector swung again, a glancing blow off the ribs. Pete connected with a left to the temple, came back with a right uppercut, and slammed another left that crushed Hector's nose.

The Apache shouted and responded with a flurry of blows. Pete raised his arms to protect his face. Hector took advantage and attacked Belissari's stomach and ribs. Belissari retreated, keeping his arms raised, letting Hector pound away. Then he dropped quickly to hands and knees. The Apache tripped over him. Pete shot up and kicked Hector in the throat.

Not hard enough. The warrior rose, although unsteadily this time, and wiped blood off his face. Pete did the same.

In the corner of his eye, he saw someone come out of the forest. An old man with a humpback, Apache for sure, carrying a red-and-black lance. He was saying something that Pete couldn't understand. Belissari knew a little of the Mescalero language, but just enough to get by to trade for a horse or sell one. Besides, his ears rang. He could barely hear anything except his hard breathing and pounding heart.

Hector noticed the Indian, too, but kept his attention on Pete. They circled again, stumbling, bleeding. The old man's voice rose. He stood only twenty yards from them now. Suddenly, Hector turned and charged the ancient Apache. Belissari took advantage. His eyes searched for his Colt or Hector's knife. He saw the corpse, the bodies of two dead horses, debris, clothes, and pelts strewn everywhere. What had gone on here? he wondered.

Then he realized what Hector was doing.

The warrior knocked the old man down, took the lance, and charged Pete. Hector let the spear sail. Belissari froze.

He would never be able to explain what happened next, no matter how many times the scene played through his mind. The lance sped toward him. His legs turned to anchors. He was a dead man. But it seemed as though a strong wind came up at that very second and blew the spear off course. But that was impossible. That would have taken a gale-force gust, or, he would sometimes think at night, something from a Homeric tale. Yet one second the lance came at his chest, and the next it sailed over his right shoulder.

Wind? Luck? Imagination? Divine intervention?

Even Hector couldn't believe what had happened. To miss with a lance at fifteen yards, throwing at a target that barely moved? Impossible.

The old man sat up and spoke again.

Hector ignored him and charged Pete.

Belissari's legs moved now. He ducked Hector's wild right, came up, drove a right into the Apache's rock-hard gut. They pounded each other.

Hector fell. Pete didn't have the strength to finish him. The Apache seemed to smile. Belissari wasn't certain for a second. Everything seemed hazy. Then the Apache sprang to his feet, and slashed away with his recovered knife.

Pete leaped back. Too late. The blade ripped through his buckskin shirt. His stomach burned. Blood trickled. Belissari dodged another swipe, lost his balance, fell, heard and felt wood snap underneath his weight.

Hector panted, grinned, said something in Apache, and came in for the kill.

Belissari's right hand gripped the piece of wood underneath him. He rolled to his knees, gripped the shaft, and brought his arm forward with all his might.

The Apache screamed.

Pete blinked and saw Hector sink to the ground, the point of the broken lance driven deep into the Indian's right thigh. The knife tumbled out of Hector's hands. He fell forward, catching himself with both hands, struggling.

Pete fought for breath.

Hector rose, on his knees, rocking. Pete swore again. Too late he saw the rock in the wounded Apache's right hand. He couldn't duck. The fist swung. Belissari's head exploded with pain.

He dropped, spread-eagled, stunned, maybe dead. He couldn't tell. Hector fell beside him with a groan.

Chapter Nineteen

He knew he was being carried into the trees, felt himself being lowered onto something soft, a robe of some kind, heard Hannah's faraway voice, realized someone was squeezing his left hand gently. Somehow he understood he lay next to Hector, out of the meadow. He tasted blood. His lungs burned. His body ached. Gentle hands raised his buckskin shirt and cleaned the shallow cut across his stomach.

Belissari opened his eyes. An ancient warrior in a shimmering helmet raised a Trojan spear over his head. His body armor, though, looked strange, as if the fighter had a humpback. The Trojan spoke to the gathering crowd.

"Hear me," the man's powerful voice roared. "let it be known throughout the land that when these two men fought in combat, Trojan against Akhaian, they gave no quarter. But afterward, they parted as friends!"

161

* * *

"Chriso mou," Hannah said with a smile.

Pete licked his lips, tried to sit up, then decided he liked it just where he was. "You're speaking Greek to me, Hannah Scott."

"I am, my sweet one. How do you feel?"

"Like I got run over by a dozen trains."

Hannah held out his canteen. He drank slowly, then nodded when he had had enough. She capped the canteen. "You look different," he said.

"You don't look like you just stepped out of Sunday school yourself. Get some rest."

He stopped her. "What happened here?" he asked. "Before I got here this morning, I mean. I heard shots."

Hannah shook her head, mumbling an "I don't know." She looked around at the Apaches huddled about, saw Hoddentin's body still in the meadow. "Someone started shooting at us," she answered. "We couldn't see who. For some reason, he stopped after you rode in. I think Sabana and Conchito went after him. They're not back yet."

Belissari knew who had fired on the Indians. "Emilio Vasquez," he whispered bitterly.

They shared their stories later that afternoon, of wintering in an Apache wickiup, of wintering in a mountain cabin, of Alv Sheerar, of Matitzal and Sabana. "I knew you were alive," Hannah said. "You wouldn't believe how, but Cynthia and I knew."

"I wasn't so sure myself for a while. Where is Cynthia?"

"I told her to run when Hector came after me.

Mountain Jay In The Juniper and her son, Napa, are looking for her now."

Pete frowned. "Nice Apache, this Hector."

"Pete," she began softly, "a lot of white men have tried to kill you and me both over the past few years. Don't blame all of the Apaches because of Hector. Besides, I'd say he has a reason to be bitter."

"You're defending him?"

"No, but I do have a big favor to ask you."

It was the dumbest idea Pete had ever heard, and he told her so. She was going to find this white-ringed mountain somewhere, if it even existed, in Mexico? She had never been south of Presidio del Norte. Absolutely not. They should persuade the Apaches to surrender to the Army at Fort Bayard or maybe Fort Bowie.

And what then? Hannah shot back. Have them ship Matitzal's people to Florida! What chance would they have there? Look at these people. They're weak. Florida would be a death sentence. No, she was going to make sure these Apaches made it to Mount Ida, with or without Petros Belissari's help.

"Mount Ida?" Pete looked bewildered. "Hannah, Mount Ida's out of Greek mythology. It's not in Mexico."

She sighed, shook her head and told Pete about her dream. Belissari didn't know what to make of it. Besides, the Bedonkohe Apaches, Hannah and Pete were trapped for the time being. Mexico seemed just as far away as Mount Ida. They were still pinned down by Vasquez, and he might have plenty of help. Where in the world was Alv Sheerar?

Hannah offered Pete a drink. He sipped it, puckered, and shook his head. Whatever it was, it certainly wasn't ouzo. Hannah called it *tizwin*. They had filled up a few gourds before leaving winter camp in the mountains. Had to, she said. Food was scarce. Pete looked around, saw the children, gaunt, dressed in rags. The old men and women looked bone-tired, half-dead. One woman with crudely cut hair sat on her knees, tears streaming down her wrinkled face, and stared at the meadow—at the body Pete had tripped over.

Hannah was right. She usually was. The Apaches would never survive Florida. He remembered the box-cars from Marfa, the ones the Army had used to transport Geronimo and his people. Matitzal's clan might not even make it to Louisiana.

"Just think about it," Hannah said, and rose. Someone was calling her. It was the chief, Matitzal. He didn't say Hannah. He said *Besdacada*.

Pete sat up, sipped some more of the miserable *tizwin*, watched Hannah stand in front of the humpbacked warrior and two other Apache men. One of those wore a funny-looking hat with pointed ears of rawhide. Another wore a sky blue headband and sleeveless shirt of pink calico. Both held battered old rifles.

"Did you find the man who shot at us?" Hannah asked Sabana.

"No. But we think he come now. He ride black horse. White flag tied to rifle barrel. I think we shoot him anyway."

"No," Hannah said. "You can't." She thought it might be Alv Sheerar, the strange man Pete had told her about. But why would he be shooting defenseless Apaches? Maybe he thought he was helping Pete rescue Cynthia and her. Or could it be the scalphunter? That seemed more likely. But why the flag of truce?

Conchito hefted his rifle. Hannah held out her hand.

"The white flag means peace," she said.

Sabana spoke to the brave, who answered curtly. "Man lying in meadow no make war," Sabana translated.

"We should hear what this man wants," Hannah said.

A voice echoed. Hannah saw the wiry man at the edge of the meadow, sitting atop a black horse and waving the white strip of cloth from his rifle barrel. The Mexican accent made her skin crawl.

"You hear this man then," Sabana said. "He ask for you anyway."

Emilo Vasquez lowered the Remington Rolling Block and grinned as Hannah walked toward him, stopping about thirty yards from the leathery scalphunter. The killer had lost his glass eye and wore a brown leather patch instead. *A cyclops,* Hannah thought. He wore shotgun chaps over his trousers, stuck in high brown boots, a Mackinaw coat and victorious expression. He pushed back his flat-brimmed hat and smiled.

"*Buenas tardes,* señorita." She heard the clicks as he thumbed back the hammer. "I almost didn't recognize you, but then I put the pieces together. So you have taken up with the Chiricahua, eh?"

"What do you want?"

"I thought of picking you off, one by one. Then this strange man rides in and fights Hector, and I came up with a better idea. Who is your white knight, Hannah Scott?"

"Pete. You didn't ans—"

"Pete Belissari? No." Vasquez laughed. "I did not recognize him. I must be getting old. Did Hector die?"

"No."

"A pity."

The horse stomped nervously. Vasquez pulled back on the reins, spoke in Spanish, refocused his attention on Hannah.

"I come with a proposal, Hannah of the Bedonkohe. I will let all of the Chiricahua, and you, go in peace. All but one. Send me Matitzal."

She remembered now. Matitzal, Vasquez had told Pete, had murdered his parents some forty years ago. The vaquero had been seeking revenge, against all Apaches, since then. Her hands felt clammy, her stomach churned, but Hannah stood her ground against this hardened killer, a murderer of women and children.

"These are my demands."

Hannah wet her lips, swallowed, replied tightly: "If you want him, why don't you go get him now?"

The scalphunter laughed. "No, no, no, señorita. If I tried this, I am afraid your Apache friends would shoot me. No, I shall wait for them to leave. Send me Matitzal. *Pronto.*"

"You have nothing to bargain with, Vasquez."

"*Sí*, I do. I have that girl of yours, the one Hector kidnapped, Cynthia, I believe is her name."

Hannah's heart jumped. Her throat went dry. Vasquez reached inside a coat pocket and withdrew a necklace. Hannah recognized the string of turquoise and rattlesnake rattles, Mountain Jay In The Juniper's gift to Cynthia.

"I do not bluff, Hannah Scott. This you know. And you know that if you do not send Matitzal to me, I will kill her."

"He won't . . . what if he . . ."

"The great leader of the Bedonkohe Apaches? He'll come. He is a man of honor. Hurry."

She tried one last ploy. "How do I know you'll let Cynthia go if Matitzal does what you ask?"

Vasquez frowned. "You don't," he said caustically, raising his voice to a high-pitched scream. "But you know I'll kill her if he doesn't!"

"That'll be hard to do, pilgrim. Yes sir, it surely will."

Hannah and the scalphunter turned to the new voice. A man sat on another black horse about a hundred yards away. He wore buckskins and the longest, wildest beard Hannah had ever seen. He pushed back a worn leather hat and spit out a mouthful of tobacco juice. He also carried a rifle in his arms. Hannah saw tiny hands clutching the fringe across the front of his shirt.

"Get down, li'l one," the man said, "hurry 'long, child. This won't take ol' Alvin Hans Sheerar any longer than it'd take to kiss a mallard."

Cynthia dropped off the horse, stumbled, fell to the ground, and got up slowly. "Mama Hannah!" she shouted, and took a couple of tentative steps forward.

"No!" Hannah found her voice. "Run, Cynthia. Run back to Matitzal."

The girl sprinted. Hannah began to back away as Vasquez turned his horse to face the newcomer, Alv Sheerar.

"Amigo," the scalphunter called out, trying to sound charming, seeing victory escape his clutches. "Amigo, there is no need for us to become enemies. I have no quarrel with you, my friend."

"But I got one with you," Sheerar called back. "Yes, sir, I most certainly got a quarrel with you. And you better savvy this: When you fit me, you ain't a-goin' up against no callow boy or innocent gal. You're ta-kin' on Alvin Hans Sheerar, and I know all about a-fightin' and a-killin', and I knows it well." He spit again. "It's fandango time, hoss. Let's dance if you got any sand, or else show me your yeller back, you miserable Mexican bushwhacker."

The buckskin-clad giant raked his spurs across the horse and charged, cutting loose with the loudest, ear-splitting, blood-curdling yell Hannah had ever heard. The black horse reared once, squealed, and charged. Vasquez swore and spurred his own horse forward to meet the challenger. Both men stuffed their reins in their mouths, raised their rifles.

Hannah dropped to her knees, thunderstruck. It was amazing, savage, wonderful, like two medieval knights jousting for the Queen's honor or the Holy Grail. Hooves pounded across the meadow. She heard shouts behind her, and realized the Apaches were cheering this display of bravery.

Two rifles roared at once, sounding like cannon fire.

Hannah shut her eyes.

Chapter Twenty

Halfway into the meadow, Pete realized he didn't have a clue as to what he thought he could do. He couldn't find his rifle or revolver. His head still hurt from the beating he had taken from Hector. Blood seeped through the bandage across his stomach where the Apache's knife had cut. Yet on he ran, or, rather, stumbled.

Cynthia raced past him, glancing at him briefly. She didn't even recognize him. He heard Alv's challenge, saw him gallop toward Vasquez, who met the charge. Hannah fell to her knees. Pete slowed down, mesmerized. The scalphunter's Remington and the mountain man's Sharps cracked as one. White smoke erupted. Two black horses crashed to the ground. Only one, Sheerar's Morgan, struggled back to its feet.

Sheerar leaped up, surprisingly quick for a man of his age and size. Vasquez shook his head, wiped a bloody lip and unsheathed his knife. They were twenty

169

yards from each other. With a laugh, the mountain man drew his D-guard Bowie. They closed in, circling each other like cocks in a fight.

Pete moved on, dreamlike, and found himself standing beside Hannah, helping her to her feet. They watched in horror and fascination. There was little else they could do.

Each man dodged a pass of the well-honed knife blades. They grunted, swung again. Vasquez laughed. "Gringo," he spoke in a raspy voice. "I shall have your scalp, too. Your mane and beard will hang above the door to my hacienda in Meoqui."

Sheerar scoffed. "Mister," he said, "you talk 'bout scalpin', but I'd lay odds that you ain't never taken no hair off nothin' 'cept possums, skunks, and puppy dogs."

The mountain man jumped back to avoid Vasquez's knife. After another minute, a few feints and jabs, the scalphunter straightened, shifting his knife into his left hand. "You bore me, old gringo," he said, reached into his coat pocket and pulled out a Remington over-and-under derringer. The tiny hideaway gun popped, and Sheerar staggered back, slapped his chest and, like the mighty Porthos, fell still.

"No!" Pete screamed, and ran toward his fallen comrade. Vasquez spun around, firing the derringer's second round. The .41-caliber slug sailed harmlessly over Belissari's head and thwacked into a tree. Vasquez tossed the empty Remington away, returned the knife to his right hand, crouched, smiled, and waited.

Pete panted, wet his swollen and busted lips, and tried to think of something. Hannah shouted. The

Apaches sang, lauding Pete's bravery, he figured, or perhaps his sheer stupidity. The blade lashed at him. He dodged the blow, sent a left into Vasquez's back as the man lunged by. The scalphunter grunted, turned, slashed again.

"Ahagahe!" came a strong voice.

Vasquez backed up a few paces. His eyes darted, careful not to take his attention off Belissari for too long. The scalphunter straightened. Now Pete chanced a look.

The humpbacked old Matitzal walked stubbornly forward, making a beeline toward Vasquez. The Apache chief kept both arms folded across his chest, his eyes dark, grizzled face full of anger.

"Ahagahe!" he shouted again. *"Ahagahe! Ahagahe!"*

Pete didn't need to understand Chiricahua to get the Indian's meaning. Old Matitzal had had enough. He was calling Emilio Vasquez out.

The scalphunter swallowed. He studied Belissari for a moment, then the motionless mountain man and Hannah.

"Ahagahe. Ahagahe. Ahagahe!"

With a savage cry, Vasquez turned and charged the chief, raising his knife over his head. "You!" the scalphunter screamed. "I cut out your heart and soul!"

Matitzal stopped, straightened as best he could, and held out his arms as if waiting to embrace a long-lost brother, or waiting to die.

On ran Vasquez, cursing, screaming, like a man struck with hydrophobia. Crazy. Frothing from the mouth. As he closed in on the patiently waiting

Apache, Vasquez stumbled. He lost control, sailed into the air, screaming with rage, and landed hard in the grass, hands under him, only three feet from the unmoving Matitzal.

With a groan, Emilio Vasquez pulled himself to his knees, weaving, choking. His right hand clutched the knife, buried to the hilt in his thin chest. The scalphunter swallowed, stared blankly at Matitzal, and with a sharp gasp, pulled out the knife. He raised his arm, bloody blade by his ear, and threw the knife at the chief. It sailed end over end, weakly, well to Matitzal's right and disappeared into the grass.

Vasquez sank down. Bleeding from the chest wound, he fell back without a sound, shuddered once, and moved no more, dead by his own hand, by his own hatred.

Matitzal nodded, turned, and walked back to his people as if nothing had happened.

The awaiting Bedonkohe Apaches broke out in song.

"You reckon it'll leave a scar, ma'am?"

Pete laughed as Hannah wrapped a bandage over Alv Sheerar's hairy chest. "The little bullet barely made a dent in your hide," Belissari said. "I thought you were dead, you old owlhoot. You took ten years off my life, you scared me so much."

Sheerar laughed. "Jehoshaphat, pilgrim. I took twenty years off my own life, and them I sure can't spare."

"You'll be fine, Mr. Sheerar," Hannah said softly.

"And the bullet might leave a scar." Not that anyone could see it through all the hair.

The Apaches looked at Alv Sheerar with fear and wonder. They called him a *gahe,* a supernatural being with curing powers who lived in the mountains. The mountain man pulled on his greasy buckskin shirt, and seeing he was the center of attention, smiled at the closest child. Napa turned, ran and leaped into his mother's arms, almost knocking her down.

Someone hurried to them. Hannah turned to see Sabana. He spoke excitedly in Apache first, caught himself, and said in English, "Bluecoats. They come. Maybe five miles away."

Hannah frowned. She almost cried. It was over. They couldn't escape now. Matitzal would have to surrender to the soldiers. Pete must have read her mind. He stood slowly, and pulled Sheerar to his feet.

"How soon can you get these people moving?" Pete asked Hannah.

They were ready now. Apaches didn't want to stay in this meadow of death. She answered. Pete looked around, saw where the Chiricahuas had strapped the dead warrior's body on his horse—no, they had thrown him on Poseidon—and were about to lead him to his final resting place. Vasquez's body lay in the valley. Pete tugged on his beard.

"You got yourself an idear, pardner?" Sheerar asked.

"Yeah, maybe." He told Hannah, "It might buy you some time."

Alv slapped Pete's back. "Let's ride, pard. I'm with you. And iffen we can't turn them cowardly bluebellies back, why we'll just have to fit 'em, you and me, pard, against the Army of the U.S. of A."

He broke into song: " 'Three hundred thousand Yankees/Be stiff as Southern dust. . . .' "

Pete reined up and looked uneasily at the bodies he pulled behind him. He couldn't quite figure out why he was doing this. Alv Sheerar chuckled and filled his mouth full of chewing tobacco.

"I thought you were out of tobacco," Pete said.

"I was. I borrowed me some offen that Mexican cuss's possibles when I rescued your li'l gal. I 'spect he don't need none where he's at. Dries your mouth out, tobaccy does."

Belissari glanced at Vasquez's body one more time before kicking his feet free of the stirrups and stretching his legs. The Army patrol slowed to a canter, then a walk. Buffalo soldiers, Pete saw. Six black troopers, a white officer, probably fresh out of West Point, and a black sergeant with a silver mustache and goatee. They circled Sheerar and Pete cautiously, horses snorting and dancing uneasily. The officer and sergeant rode forward, stopping in front of the two dirty men in buckskins.

"Second Lieutenant Henry Grey," he said, "Ninth United States Cavalry. This is First Sergeant Judd Mc-Coy."

Pete introduced himself and his partner, calling himself Buddy Pecos and Sheerar Merryweather Handal. He figured his two friends wouldn't mind the blasphemy. Grey's eyes fell on the two corpses. Belissari studied the soldiers and scout for a moment. Their clothes were caked with dust. They had been riding hard, and for a long time. The horses were winded, too, caked with sweat. This troop wasn't in any shape to go after the Apaches Pete had left behind.

"Looks like they ran into some trouble," the officer said, nodding at Hoddentin and Vasquez.

"They ran into us," Sheerar said with a laugh.

Belissari rested his hands on the saddle horn, yawned, and stretched his shoulders. *Ham it up,* he figured. *Why not?* "Lucky for us running into you all," he said. "You could save us a mess of traveling."

"How's that?" the officer inquired.

"The Apache buck is He Who Chops Off The Heads Of His Enemies—Hector, you soldiers called him. Escaped from that train back in Texas. I hear tell there's a reward for him."

Grey shook his head. "There is no reward that I am aware of, unless one was posted by the family, I mean, orphanage. The girl . . ." He looked up. "There was a girl. This Hector took a young girl hostage."

"We got her, Lieutenant. She's safe and sound."

"Where is she?"

Pete thought. He hadn't considered this. Sheerar cut in, lucky for Belissari. Pete never had been much of a liar.

"Left the gal down in Hades with her mummy, or kinda mummy, whatever it is you call a woman who runs one of them orphanage things."

"Hades?" This came from the veteran sergeant. "You left a child in Hades? Ain't there a lick of sense between you two?"

"She'll be all right," Pete interjected. He tried to

change the subject. "What brings the Army out this way?"

The officer shook his head. "First, you tell me why the Mexican is dead. Who is he?"

Pete snorted, trying to sound like a humorless killer. "Him? That's Emilio Vasquez, the scalphunter and murderer. And I know there's a bounty on his head in Mesilla."

Lt. Grey considered this. "McCoy," he said.

The sergeant dismounted and walked to the dead Indian first, lifted Hoddentin's head, examined it for a second, then let the face fall flat against Poseidon. "I reckon this is Hector, Lieutenant," he said. "Thought that Injun was younger, but you never can tell with a 'Pache." He moved to the buckskin, grabbed Vasquez's hair to lift up the head. McCoy spat. "That's Vasquez, all right. One-eyed killer. I'm glad to see him dead."

"Might be," Pete suggested, stroking his beard, "that you could file a report that you positively identified Hector and Vasquez. Make it a lot easier on us filing for that reward."

Grey thought about this. "It'll be in my report that Vasquez was positively identified. But I'm not sure about Hector."

"Lieutenant." McCoy seemed exasperated. "Who else could it be?"

The officer snapped back. "It could be one of those Apaches that were rumored to have been seen north of Lordsburg last fall. That's why we've—"

"Beggin' your pardon, Lieutenant," McCoy said, "but that's why we've been eatin' dust for the past three weeks, and that's why we haven't seen nothin' even resemblin' a 'Pache." His eyes fell on Hoddentin. "Till now, that is. This has got to be Hector, sir, so let's close the book on that killer. There ain't no more 'Paches in this country. Let's go back to Selden, sir."

Grey wiped his mouth. "Very well," he said at last. "For what it will be worth, I'll send in a report that the bodies of Emilio Vasquez and the Apache known as Hector were identified positively on this patrol. I don't know if that will help you collect your miserable bounty or not, and, frankly, I do not care." He barked out an order. "Sergeant, form a burial detail."

Pete hesitated. "Now, that's mighty friendly, sir, but Apaches have their own customs about burying—"

"Sir," Grey snapped. "You and Mr. Handal disgust me to no end. I find you as reprehensible as the two men you have slain. But the Army has pursued Hector for months now, and even Vasquez and fiends of his ilk. If you don't mind, sir, my men will have the final say in this matter. They will enjoy the satisfaction of burying these vermin."

As the troopers dug the graves, Sheerar whispered to Pete: "Seein' how you's taken a likin' to that gray mustang, pardner, you better be glad them Yanks is the ones conductin' that Cherry Cow's funeral and not the Apaches. Apaches, ol' friend, woulda killed that hoss of yourn to carry that ol' boy to the happy huntin' grounds."

Chapter Twenty-one

Much to Lt. Grey's disgust, Belissari and Sheerar camped with the soldiers that night. The next morning, the Army patrol rode southeast toward Fort Selden. Saying they were going to cut the dust in Hades before collecting their reward, Pete and Sheerar rode off to find the Apaches.

Hannah looked troubled after Pete brushed and fed the horses.

"What's the matter?" he asked.

Maybe it was the weight she suddenly felt. She didn't really know. Slowly, Hannah explained to Pete that she had hoped to have another vision, another visit from Athena, anything that could help her understand where she could lead Matitzal's clan to safety. She sighed, looking at Pete's bearded, blackened face. His brown eyes showed curiosity, maybe shock. Perhaps he looked at her as though she had lost her mind, or had turned into an Apache over the course of one winter. Maybe she had. Sometimes she felt like she was part Apache.

She shook her head.

"I don't know, Pete," Hannah finally said. "Maybe we should have let these people surrender to the government." She brushed away a tear. "I must be loco. What was I thinking? Be like Moses, lead these Apaches to the promised land? I'd wander in the desert forever." She let out a mirthless laugh. "White-ringed mountain. I am crazy."

Alv Sheerar shifted his feet.

"Did you say white-ringed mountain, ma'am?" he asked.

Of course, Alvin Hans Sheerar knew the location of a mountain down in Mexico with a white ring near the top. Why, hadn't he scouted all across that country back when he had catched the fever, or when he was marching along with Gen'ral Taylor? He knew Mexico like the back of his hand, he did, and he could find that ol' mountain in the dark, blindfolded, drunker than a goat on the worst bug juice in Hades. And he'd be plumb tickled to lead Matitzal and them folks to that mountain. Who knows? Maybe he'd find the mother lode there. And if not silver or gold, well, there were plenty of coyotes and wolves he could trap. Best bear meat he ever et came down Mexico way, too, deep in the Sierra Madres. Yep, Alvin Hans Sheerar had a hankerin' to taste some bear meat again. Good, greasy bear meat.

That's how Alv Sheerar took over as guide, chief

scout, whatever you wanted to call him. The Apaches still called him *gahe*.

They crossed the railroad tracks well east of Shakespeare in a dust storm and pushed on. Water turned scarce, but Matitzal knew where it could be found. Many white men died of thirst in this country. But not Apaches. A few days later, the Chiricahuas entered Mexico. They journeyed southward two more days before resting their stock, and plenty of sore feet.

Cynthia and the Apache children started a baseball game. Pete told Matitzal and the other men, even the silent, brooding Hector, the story of the Argonauts, translated slowly by Sabana. Hannah and Mountain Jay In The Juniper tanned a hide. Hannah tried not to notice that it was a cowhide, that Conchito had butchered some Mexican rancher's steer.

Later that evening, as Pete sat beside Matitzal and Sabana at a fire, sharing a pipe, Sheerar walked up with Hannah.

"Pardner," he said, "I've been doin' me some hard thinkin', and I reckon it's time we parted ways." He held up his right hand to head off any protest from Belissari. "No, you just sit there and think on this, pilgrim. It ain't right that you should know the location of this sacred mountain. That should be known only to these people. 'Sides that, I know that li'l gal of yourn has gots to be mighty homesick, and I'd bet all the pelts in the Rockies that you and Miss Hannah feels the same way. So come first light, I think y'all should say your good-byes and ride north. I'll take these folks home."

Pete rose. "Alv," he said, "you're not an Apache either—"

"Sure I am. They call me a *gahe*. And another thing: I already knows where this mountain is. Y'all don't."

Sabana began a quick translation. Matitzal's eyes locked on Hannah for a minute, maybe longer, then considered Pete. The chief nodded and spoke easily.

"Matitzal," Sabana interpreted, "say *gahe* right. We go on tomorrow. You go home."

Hannah helped Cynthia onto Milady before hugging Sabana. She couldn't stop the tears. Next, she kissed the mountain man's rough cheek, just above the beard, quickly, and said softly, "You're welcome in our home any time, Mr. Sheerar."

The mountain man let out a burly laugh. "You best watch yourself, Miss Hannah. I can be a pest. I taken you up on your offer, you might never get rid of me."

Pete laughed and shook the old-timer's hand. "It'd be a pleasure, pardner," he told his friend before mounting Poseidon. Belissari was ready to leave. If they didn't hurry, he would find himself crying like a newborn. "Take care of yourself, Alv," he said seriously.

Sheerar laughed. "You, too, Jim. You might be a pilgrim, but I reckon you's the bestest pardner ol' Alvin Hans Sheerar ever wintered with."

"Ready, Hannah?" Pete asked.

She nodded. "Just one more thing." Hannah stood in front of Matitzal and put her hands on the old warrior's shoulders. "You are a great leader," she said. "You told me if I led your people to Grandmother's

Country, you would give me horses. You would give me your heart. I led you to Mexico instead, to your homeland. I trust your life with my friend the *gahe*. He will take you where I couldn't." She let Sabana translate the words. Hannah was getting good at these speeches and wanted her last one to be her best. Hannah sniffed. "Know this, Matitzal. For what I have done, I do not want horses. And know this also: You will always have my heart."

She kissed him then, and backed away. Hannah wasn't sure, but she thought she saw tears well in the old man's black eyes. Maybe tears were hindering her own vision. Quickly, she put her left foot in the stirrup and pulled herself into the saddle on the buckskin.

"Let's go home," she said.

Pete stared blankly at the chief, then at Hannah. *That must have been some winter.* But, wisely, he kept his mouth shut.

Pete rested on the bench outside the Deming depot. He had sold Milady and the buckskin, and their rigs, for tickets for three people to Marfa, Texas, and passage for one gray mustang. The price he got on the tired horses and worn-out saddles and bridles wasn't great, but Pete hadn't been in a haggling mood. With the leftover money, he had treated Hannah and Cynthia to a night in the hotel, complete with hot baths, haircuts, and some store-bought duds, and a good meal, then sent a wire to Buddy Pecos in Fort Davis, informing him of their scheduled arrival in Marfa. *Bring the kids, too.* Hannah had insisted on that. Hannah and Cynthia took another bath that morning, ate breakfast at the Harvey House, went shopping, and finally came to the depot.

Belissari, on the other hand, slept in the wagon yard, still in his buckskins. He longed for a shave and a hot bath, and feared for the time when someone would attempt to comb his knotted hair before cutting it. But train tickets, telegrams, clothes, and a hotel room for one night were expensive. Pete didn't want to spend what little money remained on himself. That would wait. *I'm becoming a regular old skinflint,* he told himself. He stood, stretched, walked to the edge of the platform and looked at the sky. One o'clock, he figured. The eastbound train was due in an hour.

Hannah sat beside Cynthia, both clean and brightly dressed in calico, the child eating a peppermint stick, the woman reading a newspaper. Suddenly Hannah sat bolt upright. "Oh my gosh!"

Pete hurried to her. "What is it?" Cynthia stared excitedly, waiting, half-eaten piece of candy in her hand.

Hannah pointed at the paper. "I just noticed," she said. "It's . . . it's my birthday."

Belissari laughed, took off his hat, and scratched his unruly hair. He barely knew what month it was, let alone the date. "Shoot," he said, "if I had known that I would have bought you a present." He didn't consider the clothes and hotel amenities gifts.

Cynthia giggled. "You should kiss her, Pete."

Hannah stood stiffly at the thought. Pete quickly realized she didn't look happy about the idea. He stepped closer to her.

"You are not kissing me, Petros Belissari," she said firmly.

Belissari contemplated. "Why not?"

"You need a bath, Petros. You're filthy. Not only that, I've never kissed you with a full beard, especially one that dirty. You might have lice."

"No, I don't have lice. I admit I can use a bath, but it is your birthday, and it's still me," he said.

"It's your voice. It isn't your face."

This conversation sounded vaguely familiar. He looked at Hannah, recognized the determination in her eyes, then glanced at Cynthia, grinning mischievously, face stained by the candy.

"Kiss her anyway, Pete!"

Pete dropped his hat and swept a screaming Hannah Scott into his arms. She protested, but not too much.

Author's Note

Although primarily written as a fantasy, as are all novels in this series, *The Odyssey of Hannah and the Horseman* has some basis in fact that might interest the reader.

After the end of the Indian wars in Arizona in 1886, the Apaches, including so-called hostiles along with Army scouts, were exiled as prisoners of war to Alabama and Florida. One Warm Springs brave named Massai, however, escaped the transport train near St. Louis and somehow eluded the Army to return to his home country, where he hid out for some twenty-five years before disappearing into history and Apache lore.

Other Apaches also never surrendered. As late as the 1930s and '40s, clans were found living deep in the mountains of Mexico. Sadly, many of these were tracked down and slaughtered, reminiscent of the days of government-backed scalphunters.

185